A King Production presents…

By

Joy Deja King

ISBN 10: 1-942217-28-5
ISBN 13: 978-1942217282
Author: Joy Deja King
Cover concept by Joy Deja King & www.MarionDesigns.com
Cover Model: Joy Deja King
Typesetting: Linda Williams
Edited by: Dolly Lopez & Linda Williams

Library of Congress Cataloging-in-Publication Data; King, Deja
Queen Bitch: a novel/by Joy Deja King
For complete Library of Congress Copyright info visit;
www.joydejaking.com

A King Production
P.O. Box 912, Collierville, TN 38027

A King Production and the above portrayal log are trademarks of A King Production LLC

Dedication

This Book is dedicated To My Family,
Readers and Supporters.
I LOVE you guys so much.
Please believe that!!

Acknowledgments

What's up everybody!! I'm so excited about Queen Bitch. This is truly my favorite installment of the Bitch Series so far. Precious started off having nothing and worked her way up to having it all. I had no choice but to take it all away because only then, can you learn to appreciate your blessings.

Tazzy, my reader extraordinaire; it's nothing like getting your stamp of approval on one of my productions. Tureko "Virgo" Straughter, Trista Russell, Lady J, Ms KiKi, Andrea Denise, Sunshine716, Ms.(Nichelle) Mona Lisa, Lady Scorpio, Travis Williams, Brittney, Donnell Adams, Myra Green, Leona Romich, Sexy Xanyell. Also, to vendors, and distributors like African World Books, Black & Nobel, DCBookman, Tiah, Vanessa and Glenn Ledbetter, Afriqiah Books, Cyrus Webb, Ann Hopson and Rahman

Muhammad…thank you all for your support!!

Special thanks to Cover 2 Cover Book Club; Christian Davis, Angela Slater, Pamela Rice, Ahmita Blanks, Melony Blanks, Marcia Harvey, Melinda Woodson, Tonnetta Smith, Tiffany Neal, Miisha Fleming, Tamika Rice and Bar. I so enjoyed our book chats for Hooker to Housewife and Superstar. All of you ladies are wonderful!!

Special, special thanks to Linda Williams; you really came through for me. I LOVE your skills!! Not only are you super talented at what you do but you have a beautiful heart. Tracy Taylor, Sherita Redic-Nunn, Keith Saunders of Marionsdesigns and Jonesy!!

Much Love
Joy Deja King

A KING PRODUCTION

Queen BITCH

Part 4

JOY DEJA KING

Precious
On Everything I Love

God, protect me from my friends. I can handle my enemies. I never forgot reading that in the front pages of a novel. Those words resonated with me. At the time I read it, I didn't believe it applied to me because I had no friends, that was, until I took Maya under my wing. Now here I was, shackled up in a dreary basement, sitting on the cold cement floor with the person I considered being like my own blood staring down at me. No, she wasn't the anointed sister I never had, she was my worst enemy. I had let my guard down, and got caught slipping. Now this diabolical heifer wanted me to step out my shoes and give them to her, then hand her the keys to my cars and house so she could live in that too. To say this chick had me jammed up would be an understatement.

"Maya, you need to go 'head and slit my throat, put a bullet through my heart or however your trife ass wanna take me out, 'cause I ain't helping you take my husband. I wouldn't wish you on the worse nigga I fucked, let alone Supreme."

"Bitch, you think I'm playing wit' your stupid ass? When I said I would take your daughter out this world, I meant it!" Maya said with so much vengeance that spit sprayed out her mouth after each word. Then to make sure I got her message Maya balled up her fist and clocked me on the side of my left temple, causing my eyes to lock shut and my head to plummet down in pain. "Those are the exact type of licks your precious Aaliyah will be getting if you don't wise up and get with the plan."

This ho is truly fuckin' crazy. How in the hell did I get blindsided and not see I was dealing with a mental case? I believe this sick motherfucker might really kill my baby. I ain't taking no chances. I'll play along with her ass while I'm plotting to get the fuck up outta here and send this bitch floating in the Pacific Ocean somewhere.

"You made your point, Maya. I'll do whatever I have to do," I said, containing the rage I wanted to spew on her.

"Good, that's a smart decision. Since you can't save your own life at least you can save that of your daughters'."

"I guess that's your slick way of letting me know I'ma dead bitch once you don't need me anymore."

"But of course. I thought that was already understood. Once we have our fun with you, it's a wrap.

Until then, I promise we'll take good care of you. On that note, I must be going." Maya looked down at her watch. "I'm sure Supreme is starting to wonder where you are and of course I must be there to begin planting my seeds."

"It's not too late for you to dead this shit, Maya. You, your brother and the third stooge, Devon, can get out of town."

"And what, let you go free? After all the hard work we've put in, to hatch this plan? That just ain't gonna happen."

Maya was determined to see this shit through and there was nothing I could do but figure out a way to break the fuck out, which under the current circumstances was damn near looking impossible. After the punch Mike landed on my jaw and the fist Maya branded on my temple, trying to concoct an escape plan had my head triple spinning in pain. I could barely keep my eyes open and wanted to succumb to my need to pass out, but when I saw Mike grab Maya's arm and pull her to the side, I willed myself to focus.

"Maya, you need to chill with all this talk about hurting the baby. That shit ain't cool. I know you want Precious to cooperate with you, but you going overboard with pretending you would hurt an innocent child, especially one that might be our blood," Mike said in a low but stern voice as if he didn't want me to hear him.

"Shit, I ain't fucking pretending," Maya boasted loudly, making it clear she didn't give a fuck who was privy to her threats. "That was some real talk," she continued.

"Maya, keep your fucking voice down!" Mike ordered, grabbing the bottom of her elbow and edging her forward.

Maya yanked her arm away, showing her displeasure of her brother's manhandling. "You getting yourself all worked up over a child that probably ain't even yours."

"Well, until we know for sure let's put a cease to all the baby threats. Is that understood?" Maya remained silent with a blank stare. "Are we clear." Mike barked loudly making more of a statement than asking a question.

"You can relax, I got you, dear brother," Maya finally said, releasing herself from Mike's clutch. "I really have to go. I don't need any suspicions falling on me."

"That's cool. So I guess I'll see you back here tomorrow?"

"Yeah, if everything's straight. Devon, you need to be leaving shortly too. I don't want Supreme to have problems tracking you down."

"I feel you. I'm 'bout to break out."

"A'ight gentlemen, I'll be in touch. Oh, and have a goodnight, Precious. I'll make sure to give Aaliyah a kiss for you." Both Mike and I gave Maya a look of disgust, but she sauntered out like she could give a fuck.

"Can I get a blanket, pillow, something? It's cold as shit down here," I asked Mike trying to vibe him out.

"What the fuck you think this is, the penthouse suite? The only thing you getting from me is bread and water," he said, coldly.

"Oh, so all that talk about taking good care of me until it was checkout time was some bullshit?"

"Letting your ass live a little bit longer is taking good care of you. Be happy you getting that."

"Like I said from jump, under these conditions you would be doing me a favor by killing me now. It's your sister that wants to keep me alive for her own twisted reasons."

"Maybe, but I like the idea of letting you suffer a bit before ending your life. Being locked up like an animal is one of the most humiliating feelings in the world, especially when you a rich nigga used to living a life of luxury. You can get a taste of how I felt being locked up at Clinton for all that time. I'ma enjoy watching your Beverly Hills ass being dead on the inside but very much alive on the outside, to see how pathetic you'll be when we're done with you."

I simply put my head down and ignored what Mike said. There was no sense riling him up any further because whatever torture plan they had in mind, I prayed it didn't include Mike raping me again.

"I'm outta here, Mike. I'll check in tomorrow," Devon said, giving Mike a pound. He had been so damn quiet, I almost forgot he was still in the room. My eyes darted around the chilly, dark basement which I would now be calling home for however long. At any moment I expected a rat to dash across the concrete floor or a poisonous spider to crawl up my leg. I was truly in hell.

"Hold up, I'll follow you up. I'm done with her for the day," Mike said, grabbing some keys off a metal chair in the center of the room. "Sleep tight, Precious. And don't bother screaming because this room is soundproof. Plus, we way the fuck out, can't nobody find you here anyway."

I watched as Mike and Devon went upstairs leaving me alone in this miserable existence as if I was nothing. I stared up at the small dim light bulb dangling from the ceiling, hoping that one day I would see the light again too. Then I heard the door slam and my body jumped, and a few seconds later it was pitch dark.

"I can't believe they turned off the little bit of light I had." My body stiffened up in fear not able to see shit. "On everything I love, all those motherfuckers gon' pay!"

Maya
Good Girl Gone Bad

As I pulled up my candy apple red Jaguar to the gates, a smile crept across my face. I knew that if I played my cards right that soon this estate and everything in it would belong to me, including Supreme.

"Hey, Maya," the security guard waved as he opened the gate for me. I simply grinned and waved back. I remembered that he was one of the only guards that Precious liked, and I made a notation to myself to fire his ass after I became the new Mrs. Mills.

As I drove up the circular entrance and parked near the waterfall, it was time for me to put my game face on. Once Supreme got wind that Precious was missing he would instantly suspect foul play. Every movement I made from the moment I stepped through the front door would then be critiqued, so from the get, I had to come correct.

I took a deep breath and headed to the door using my key for entry. Before I had a chance to close it, Aaliyah came running towards me. I assumed she had been expecting her mother the way her sparkly eyes and bubbly smile instantly disappeared when she realized it wasn't Precious.

"Hi, Aaliyah!" I gushed, bending down on my knees and giving her a hug. She reciprocated the affection but it wasn't the excitement she always had when greeting her mother.

"What up, Maya? We thought you were Precious," Supreme said, walking towards us in the forty-foot high limestone entry.

"Precious isn't here? Where did she go?"

"She left early this morning to pick up a surprise she had for me, and here it is going on five o'clock and I haven't heard from her."

"You haven't heard from her since this morning? That's strange. Did you try her cell?"

"Yeah, I been blowing that shit up but she ain't answering her cell or the car phone. You haven't heard from her either?"

"You know how I'm always forgetting my cell. I left it in my bedroom. Let me go check to see if she left me a message."

"Thanks, I appreciate that, Maya."

"No problem, but I'm sure she'll be walking through the front door any moment," I said, giving Aaliyah a kiss before heading upstairs. When I got to my bedroom I closed the door and took my cell

out of my purse, tossing it on the bed. I sat down
for a few minutes letting some time pass to give the
impression I was checking my calls. But before I
could even make it back downstairs Supreme was
knocking on my door.

"Maya," I heard Supreme call out after beginning a
second round of banging.

"Come in." I flipped my cell open pretending to be
checking messages. I held a finger up giving Supreme
a sign to wait as if listening intently. "Nothing," I sighed
shutting my phone close.

"Damn, this shit is crazy. Where could she be?"

"Supreme, I'm positive she's good. Precious
probably decided to get a spa treatment at the last
minute and lost track of time, you know, some simple
bullshit like that."

"Maybe you're right. She is good for getting side-
tracked."

Ring…Ring…Ring!

"Hold on, Maya, let me get that. It might be Precious
calling."

"Go head, it probably is…*not!*" I chuckled as
Supreme rushed to pick up the landline. It was a
shame the circles Supreme would be running around
in for the next few weeks, wondering where the hell
his wife was. I damn sure didn't want to see him
losing his mind over Precious' useless ass, but shit
had to run its course.

I decided to head in Supreme's direction to give
the notion of concern for Precious whereabouts. At
first I walked towards their master bedroom, but

then realized the sound of his voice was coming from downstairs. By the time I reached the bottom step, Supreme's once calm voice had now raised and become animated.

"What you mean she never came to pick it up? That was hours ago and you just now calling! Fuck that! I don't want to hear none of your fucking excuses. This is some bullshit! I'm on my way over there!" Supreme roared before slamming the phone down.

"Supreme, who was that?"

"The fucking jewelry store where Precious was supposed to be picking up something for me. They said she never showed up."

"What? She was supposed to have done that hours ago!"

"I know, and the only reason those dumb fucks called was because she was supposed to pay the remaining balance once she picked up the shit, and they worried about getting their damn money."

"So what are you going to do?"

"I'm going over there and see what the fuck is up."

"Well, I'm coming with you."

"Cool, let me go tell Anna we're heading out."

My mind began racing because I hadn't thrown in the mix the possibility of the jewelry store calling and Supreme being alerted so soon that shit was shady. *Remain calm Maya. This ain't nothing but a minor bump that isn't gonna change shit in the plan.*

"A'ight, let's go," Supreme said, shaking me out my thoughts as I followed him to the Maybach waiting out front. "Where's Devon?" Supreme asked the driver who was standing out front and opened the back door for us.

"Mr. Mills, he got held up but said he would be here shortly. He asked me to stay on until he arrived."

Oh shit! I told Devon dumb ass not to get missing. That motherfucker better have his story airtight when Supreme grill him on why the fuck he was late for his shift.

"I'll deal with that nigga later. Head over to Cartier on Rodeo Drive," Supreme directed the driver. He then hit a button on his phone and kept redialing the same number over and over again, and I assumed it was Precious'.

"Who are you are calling?" I asked innocently.

"Who the fuck you think I'm calling? My wife!" Supreme snapped.

"I'm sorry, that was a dumb question." I opted to remain silent for the rest of the ride because Supreme was in full blaze mode right now, and one wrong word, he might have the driver pull over and tell me to get the fuck out the car.

"Don't go to the lot, pull up right in front," Supreme said and hopped out before the driver could even put the car in park.

I slid over to get out on Supreme's side, but he slammed the door in my face. I leaned back over to my side and got out trying to remain close on Supreme's tail. When I entered Cartier passing the red velvet rope, Supreme was already at the counter demanding to see the manager. It was my first time in the store, but instantly I felt at home. The over 900 square foot of retail space, two level boutique had endless decorative touches—from heavy drapes to an 800 pound Murano glass chandelier designed to make the place feel very intimate. Everything from the carpet to curtains was like what you would find in a private residence.

"Yes, Sir, I'm the manager. How may I help you?" a short cropped, dark haired gentleman asked in a funny English accent.

"I got a call from one of your salespeople about an item my wife was supposed to pick up from here earlier today."

Then a snotty, painfully thin bottled blond white chick whispered something in the manager's ear. He simply nodded his head while Supreme leaned on the glass counter as if he was about to smash his elbow through it.

"Yes, Mrs. Mills was supposed to be picking up some items we had costumed made for her. Are you here to pay the remaining balance?"

"Listen, ain't nobody tripping off your little remaining balance. I want to know what time my wife was supposed to pick up the jewelry, who spoke to her last, and what did she say."

"No need to get upset, sir. We appreciate your business and would be more than happy to assist you with your questions, but we do need to be paid for the items your wife ordered. These are specialty items and cannot be resold, that is why we were concerned about receiving the remaining balance."

"Yo, would you please stop beating me in the head about that fucking remaining balance? I heard you the first fucking time when you clowns called my crib! What, because I'ma nigga you think me and my wife can't afford to pay for the shit?"

The manager's face turned beet red.

"Supreme, calm down," I said putting my hand on his shoulder.

"Don't fucking tell me to calm down!" Supreme jerked his shoulder, blowing my hand away. A few other customers in the store and the security guard up front were all focusing their attention in our direction.

"That man looks awfully familiar. Is he some sort of actor or something?" I overheard one middle aged white woman say to her male counterpart as they browsed the accessories section.

"Sir, I'm going to need you to calm down," the manager pleaded.

"Or what, you're going to call the police? Go 'head, then you'll neva get that remaining balance."

"Then we would have to take legal action."

"Sue me, you bootleg Mr. Belvedere, 'cause I have *big* lawyers. So you can either answer my questions and get your fucking remaining balance, or you can keep annoying me with that damn fake ass English accent and get nothing!"

The manager let out a deep sigh. "Carol, who spoke to Mrs. Mills today?"

"I did," the painfully thin sales clerk answered.

Supreme then put his glare on her. "When?" he asked.

Carol turned her head to her manager as if waiting for his approval before she answered. He nodded his head indicating it was okay to speak and she continued. "I spoke to Mrs. Mills yesterday evening before we closed, and then this morning around ten o'clock. She said she was on her way and would be here shortly. That is why I decided to call her home because I had been waiting and she never showed up," Carol said, in that same funny English accent as her boss.

"So what took you so long to call the crib if you spoke to her around ten? It's about to be six o'clock," Supreme said, agitated.

"Sir, I had been calling her cell phone and left several messages, as that was the primary number she gave. I then realized she also left a secondary number and that is when I called."

"Damn, you shoulda seen that shit sooner. All this time has passed and I don't know what could've happened to her. Maybe some foul shit." Supreme said with distress in his voice.

"Mr. Mills, how were we supposed to know that something unfortunate could've happened to your wife?" the manager interjected before Carol could say another word.

"I understand that, but it still doesn't change the fact that I haven't heard from my wife since she left this morning to come to your store." Supreme put his head down staring as if transfixed on something he could see through the glass cases. Everyone remained frozen, not knowing what to do or say next.

"Sir, would you like to see your wife's purchases?" Carol finally asked, trying to melt the ice and, I'm sure to collect their dough. I was worried Supreme was going to choke hold the broad for once again mentioning the items, but surprisingly Supreme seemed serene about seeing them. The woman walked behind a closed door and came out with two long red velvet boxes. She placed them on top of the countertop before opening each one up.

I stepped forward wanting to get an up close inspection of the jewels. "Precious, always had spectacular taste," I mumbled under my breath, taking in the jewelry.

"It's his and hers cuff link white diamond bracelets. The emblematic Cartier link is borrowed from the Maison's cult animal, the panther collection. As you can see the diamond paving pieces are sensually wrapped around and the fluid lines sparkle with the light of a thousand flames," Carol gave her spill extra eloquently as her boss smiled in approval. I couldn't be mad at the bitch for keeping to her sales pitch even though it was evident her would be customer was more than pissed the fuck off.

"Your wife also had the inside engraved. Here, take a look." Carol slid the bracelet closer to Supreme so he could inspect it. "It says 'Love 4 Life...Always'. That's beautiful."

I was ready to spit on Carol's toothpick ass by this particular point. She was spreading the romantic bullshit on a little too thick. All I needed was for some motherfuckers to step out playing their violins.

"Here, just bag it up for me," Supreme said, placing his American Express Centurion—also known as

the Black Card—on the glass top. My mouth began
salivating at the thought of Supreme using that
very credit card on me as I devoured Rodeo Drive,
shutting the stores down.

Carol and her manager's face lit up as she swiped
Supreme's card through the machine, collecting his
coins. "Here's your receipt, sir, and it was a pleasure
doing business with you and your wife," Carol said.

"And Mr. Mills, I'm sure Mrs. Mills is fine," the
manager added with an optimistic smile. Supreme
simply grabbed the bag and receipt and said nothing.

I walked slowly behind Supreme trying to get a read
on his body language. I couldn't tell if he was angry,
worried, or suspect of me. Until I was sure I decided to
remain mute. When we got outside the driver stepped
out the Maybach and opened the door for Supreme
and I to get in, but suddenly Supreme halted his stride.
Without saying a word he handed the Cartier bag to his
driver and sprinted off. I tried to stay within proximity
to see what the fuck was going on without appearing
to damn nosey.

"Oh fuck!" I said under my breath once I got a
view of what had Supreme dashing off.

"Get this fucking car off the back of your tow truck!"
Supreme screamed, banging on the driver side window.

The man was at a stop light about to pull off before
Supreme rolled up on him, and I wished he had. "Man,
what the hell is wrong with you?" the young black man
said, rolling down his window. "How you going to
bang on my window in the middle of the street?"

"Pull this truck over!" Supreme demanded, not caring

that the light had now turned green and he was holding up traffic.

"Man, I'm on the job. I ain't pulling shit over."

"This my motherfucking car you got latched on the back of your shit and I want to know where the fuck you got it from." Now horns were blowing and people were sticking their heads out of their cars telling them to move, but Supreme didn't budge.

"Supreme, what's going on? You're holding up traffic," I said, trying to sound like the voice of reason.

"I don't give a fuck!" he said, grabbing the tow truck driver's collar and pulling him so close that their noses were an inch away from touching. "Pull this fucking truck over, now!"

Right when I believed Supreme was about to start laying blows we heard police sirens pulling up. Supreme pushed the man back, getting his composure together, but the dude began getting all extra for the cops.

As one cop began directing the traffic the other officer began interrogating Supreme and the driver. "Both of you put your hands up!" he ordered, wanting to make sure neither was armed. "What is going on here? The two of you are holding up traffic."

"Officer, this man came up to me out of nowhere banging on my window and demanding me to pull over acting crazy. Then this idiot tells me this is his car, like he can afford a half a million dollar custom made Lamborghini," he said, in a cynical voice, turning towards Supreme. He then turned back towards the officer and did a quick glance back at Supreme. "Oh

shit!" The man paused as if getting a good look at the
person who was ready to put an ass whooping on him
a minute ago. "Oh shit!" he repeated. "You Supreme!
What the fuck, music mogul Supreme just tried to jack
me up! My fault, man. I didn't realize it was you," he
said, with a big ass Kool-Aid smile.

Supreme stood shaking his head in frustration.

"I don't care who he is, you can't hold up traffic.
Now pull this truck over to the side so we can
clear this matter up," the officer directed.

"Listen, officer. I just left the Cartier store because
my wife was supposed to come by earlier and pick
up some jewelry, but she never got there. When I
was leaving the store I noticed the car she had been
driving when she left this morning on the back of
the tow truck. I wanted to know where he got the
car from in hopes that it could give me a clue as to
where my wife might be."

"Hold on a minute. What is your name?" the officer
asked, taking out his notepad.

"Xavier Mills."

"So you believe your wife is missing?"

"I don't know, but something ain't right."

"And who are you?" the officer asked, turning his
question on me.

"Maya. I'm a friend of his wife, Precious."

"And I assume a friend of her husband too?"

"Yes, we're both concerned about her whereabouts."

The officer nodded his head and jotted something
down on his notepad.

"Listen, can we please go speak to the driver? I

need to know where he picked up my car from."

"You stay here. I'll go speak with the tow truck driver, and when I'm done I'll then speak to both of you. Excuse me."

"Yo, these cops get on my fucking nerves. They wanna be so by the fucking *book* when it's convenient for them."

"Supreme, I know it's hard but try to relax."

"I can't fucking relax until I find out what happened to my wife!"

"We will find her. I'm sure she's okay."

"Nah, I gotta bad feeling about this," Supreme said, shaking his head as he ran his hand over his face. "God help me if Precious isn't okay, because if she's not, I'm done."

Then done is what Supreme would be, because Precious wasn't okay and never would be again, thanks to me. But who could really fault me for my actions. I mean, all is fair in love and war, and like a true friend, I would be right there to help Supreme pick up the pieces to his broken heart. Most would call my tactics ruthless or maybe just a good girl gone bad.

Precious

Work In Progress

"It's morning, now wake the fuck up!" Mike yelled in my face as I struggled to open my eyelids. I had only managed to fall asleep a couple of hours ago and now this fool was bringing me back into my misery.

"Damn, I'm finally able to get some sleep and here you come waking me up."

"I'm doing you a favor."

"How you figure that?"

"You know they say sleep is the cousin of death," Mike said, bending down to eyelevel so we were facing each other. "Now I'm sure you need to use the bathroom, so I brought this for you."

I looked at the large plastic cup and back at Mike.

"What, you expect me to piss in that?"

"This, or you can piss on yourself, It's up to you."

"Did you at least bring me some tissue?"

"But of course," he said, reaching behind him and placing the tissue next to the red plastic cup. "Now listen carefully, because if you fuck this up, I'ma have to fuck you up."

"I'm listening."

"I'm going to unlock one of the handcuffs on your wrist so you can do your thing."

"Oh, and I just assumed you were going to wipe my pussy for me after I pissed," I said, sarcastically.

"Cute, but don't get cute when I take off this handcuff, because it won't be a good look for you."

"I got you."

"Now when you're finished, place the cup to the side and put this top on there."

"I don't understand why you don't let me use the bathroom. I mean you can't expect me to shit in this cup too, now can you?" I asked mockingly.

"Ain't nobody expecting you to shit in this cup. Just do what I tell you when I tell you. I'm handling this. I know you used to being in control, but that's your past and we dealing with the present."

"Point made. But um, can you turn around and give me some privacy?"

"Oh please! I've seen everything you got, remember?"

"How can I forget? You did rape me!"

"Why don't you admit it, Precious?"

"Admit what?"

"That you wanted it. That tight pussy was hot for me."

"This cup can't hold my piss and vomit, and that's what I'm about to do if you keep on with that repulsive shit."

"Now, now, now, how soon we forget. You were practically begging for the dick when you had your legs spread open and I finger fucked you on the mahogany desk in your den."

"That was before I knew what a sick monster you are and that you were responsible for trying to have my husband killed."

"Those are all minor things and it still doesn't change the fact that you wanted me just as much as I wanted you."

"Will you please just turn around?" I waited for a few seconds and Mike finally turned his back towards me. It was some uncomfortable shit trying to squat down to piss with one wrist in a handcuff and shackles on your legs, but I managed.

As I was finishing up I eyed Mike contemplating if there was anyway I could make a move that could get me the fuck out of here. He was a few feet away from me and I could see the keys to the locks in his hand. I wondered, if I could get him closer and toss the urine in his face and then maybe use my fingers to dig in his eyes, would that give me enough time to somehow grab the keys, unchain myself and break out? Shit, under my current conditions I had nothing to lose.

I gripped the rim of the cup firmly, seriously pondering the scheme I had devised in my head. Although it seemed like a long shot, I was ready to take my chance...that was until we got company.

"Good morning, dear brother," Maya said, strolling down the stairs. With Maya in the room I knew I would have to revisit my escape plan another time.

"What's good? I wasn't expecting you this early."

"I know, but I'm going to be a busy bee today, so I wanted to check in with you as early as possible."

"I feel you. How's it going on over there in Supreme's household? I'm sure by now he's wondering why his wife hasn't come the fuck home," Mike chuckled, smiling in my direction.

"Poor Supreme isn't taking it very well. And it didn't help that you idiots left the fucking car in the parking lot by Cartier. Why didn't you move that shit?"

"Maya, we didn't have time for all that. We were trying to get in and out without raising any sort of suspicion."

"Don't you think it looks suspicious that you left her vehicle by a store that she never went into?"

"That was the best place to grab shorty. Wasn't nobody around and we figured it would take a minute for anybody to notice the car sitting there. But shit, at least we grabbed her cell and tossed that shit. If we had left it at the scene it would've really looked like some foul play. She could've parked her car there and decided to bounce. Don't nobody know for sure."

"Damn! Could the two of you please stop talking about me like I ain't sitting right here?" I said, getting exhausted just listening to their bickering.

"As far as I'm concerned you ain't here unless I need you for some shit," Maya retorted like she was some bigwig.

"Fuck all that! How did Supreme find the car and

what happened after that?" Mike butted in, wanting to get down to the facts and not dwelling on Maya's fiction.

"Cartier called wanting to know why Precious hadn't come to pick up her shit, and when Supreme and I left the store he saw a tow truck taking the car away. So that turned into a big production. He ended up filing an unofficial missing person's report with the police officer and then speaking with the driver of the tow truck."

"What you mean 'unofficial' report?" Mike questioned, and my ears were burning up extra hard hoping my husband was on the case and not falling for Maya's slick ass innocent role.

"You know, technically you're supposed to have to wait twenty-four hours before filling a missing person's report. But the officer went ahead and took it because of the whole car episode. That's why I'm pissed that you all didn't dump that shit somewhere."

"Get the fuck over it. Our priority was snatching up Precious and that's what we did. All that other shit is immaterial."

"You may not care, but I'm the one who has to keep Supreme under control. This nigga already flipping and he ain't even found a body or no shit."

"What did you expect, Maya? I'm his wife, the mother of his child. Of course he's flipping, and he gonna be doing a lot more than that when he finds out your knee-deep in this shit."

"Bitch, please! You ain't the end all be all. The same way he was getting pussy before he met you, he'll be getting it after you, so let me worry about Supreme."

"Maya, can you get off Supreme's dick for one second and tell me the move that nigga tryna make next?"

Maya gritted her teeth and rolled her eyes at Mike, obviously agitated that he wasn't a supporter over her obsession with Supreme. I figured right then that the only way I even had a slight chance of getting out of here was using Mike's hatred towards Supreme to my advantage, but how to do it was the difficult part. One thing was for sure and two for certain, Mike Owens was not to be underestimated, and he was no dummy. In fact, he was one of the smartest men I had ever encountered. That's why it was such a fucking waste that he was a complete sociopath."

"Real talk, he playing his shit close to the vest."

That's right baby, shut that trifling ho down! I smiled to myself.

"He definitely believes there has been some foul play involved, but he isn't sharing with me what or who he thinks is responsible. I don't want to pry too much and then bring suspicion on me. I'm playing it cool."

"That's the smart way to move, but still find a way to stay on top of his shit. You don't want any unexpected surprises."

"I got you."

"Is Devon coming over today?"

"I doubt it. Supreme was mad skeptical when we left to go to Cartier yesterday and Devon hadn't arrived for his shift. That's why I had told that motherfucker not to get missing."

"Was he able to smooth shit over with Supreme?"

"I think so. When we got back home Devon was there and gave him some excuse about some emergency coming up with his girl. Supreme seemed to have bought it, but I told Devon to stay within sniffing distance of Supreme until shit mellow out."

"That's cool. And how's Aaliyah?" Mike questioned, actually sounding genuinely concerned.

"She's doing fine."

"I know she must be wondering where her mother is."

"Yeah, but kids are resilient. She'll get over it," Maya shrugged.

I tried to stay out of their conversation, but hearing Aaliyah's name made my blood start bubbling. "No she's mot gonna get over it! She ain't a puppy, Maya, she's my little girl!"

"*Was* your little girl."

"It don't matter what you do to me, Aaliyah will always be my child and ain't nothing gonna change that."

"I'm so sick of hearing your self righteous jabber. Maybe if I take this," Maya snarled as she reached towards my neck, ripping my pink diamond necklace off, "You'll shut the fuck up and acknowledge that little happy family life you were living is now over."

A shiver shook through my body and I looked down at my bare neck. That necklace was a symbol of the love and bond that I shared with Supreme. The last and only time I had been without it was when Mike took it off my neck that night he raped me. And now Maya was raping me again when she snatched it off.

"You're going to burn in hell for that, Maya!"

"You talking a lot of shit for someone who is already living there. Huh, and you stink! Mike, give this bitch a bath. I have to go and check on my man, Supreme anyway." Maya was doing her best to rub it in my face that I was without my child and my husband.

I felt a tear beating to drop out of my eye, but I refused to let it fall. I would not let that trick or her brother know they were breaking me. I took a deep breath and swallowed hard, getting pumped up.

"I ain't the only one who needs a bath!" I mocked, tossing the cup of piss I was still holding in her face. "Now who stink?"

At first Maya was so stunned by what I did she wasn't sure what I had thrown on her, but then the stench kicked in and she was incensed. "Heffa, I'ma kill you right now!" Maya howled as she lunged at me.

Mike rushed over to block Maya from unleashing her beat down as I used my one free hand to try to get some licks in. "Maya, chill!"

"Don't tell me to chill! I'ma fuck her up!" Maya continued screaming and swinging her arms.

"I'll handle Precious. You go clean yourself up."

Maya stayed eyeing me with flames sprouting from her head. I stared right back and even cracked a smile, happy to have been given a chance to fuck her day up the way she had been fucking up mine.

"I ain't done with you!" Maya warned as Mike walked her piss-soaked ass up the stairs.

My insides were dancing around and doing

cart-wheels, thrilled that I had put the bitch in her place if only for a few minutes.

By the time Mike came back from walking Maya upstairs I had eliminated my joyous smile and put back on my stoic exterior.

"I was planning on giving you a decent meal today, but after that shit you pulled that's dead," Mike said, locking my free hand back in the handcuff.

"It was worth it. Maya deserved that shit and then some."

"Let's see if you feel that way when all you get is a biscuit for breakfast, lunch and dinner. But on the real," Mike said with a frown, "You are a bit funky, so I'ma take you upstairs so you can shower."

"Wow, I get a bath! Why do you even care what I look or smell like?"

"Shit, I gotta look at your ass everyday for at least the next couple of weeks. I prefer for you to be decent."

"Why are you going to keep me alive for at least the next couple of weeks?"

"Mind your business. Like I said, I'm in control."

"If you're so in control, how can you allow your sister to talk about Aaliyah that way? Especially when you know there is a possibility that she could very well be your daughter." I caught Mike off guard with that and he didn't know how to come back at me. His jaws began flinching and nostrils flaring. I wanted to get the nigga worked up and felt he had opened the door, so I decided to kick it in. "Oh, you stumped for words. Maya working you like she running the show and disrespecting your seed like you a clown nigga. I mean what's really good?"

"Yo, shut the fuck up! Maya ain't running shit."

"Then how you gonna allow her to threaten to hurt Aaliyah?"

"Maya is all talk. She would never hurt an innocent child. We brutal, but not like that. I warned her about the Aaliyah threats and you see she stopped."

"Yeah, she stopped in front of you, but you don't have any clue what Maya's doing when she get behind closed doors and is alone with her."

"Precious, I know what you're trying to do, and I'm not feeding into that bullshit. If Aaliyah is my daughter, not only will I guarantee not even so much as a hair on her head will be harmed, but she will also grow up with *me*."

"Excuse me, how in hell will you pull that off, given that you're an escaped convict."

"You always dwelling on the minor obstacles. I'm into doing major shit. Now marinate on that while I go check on Maya."

I let out a sigh of revulsion watching Mike leave. The idea of him raising Aaliyah was nauseating. Mike was a wanted man, and the only way he could raise Aaliyah was if he left the country. Without a doubt in my mind that was exactly what the motherfucker planned on doing after I was dead and out the picture. Knowing the clock was ticking with time not being on my side, I was intent on finding a way to turn brother against sister. But there was no denying that it would be over my dead body to let that scenario come to fruition. I had already begun planting the seeds and it was still a work in progress.

Maya

No Clue...Clueless

"I can't believe that bitch threw her nasty ass piss on me!" I kept belting out loud as I drove home. Luckily I always kept an extra set of clothes, shoes and other feminine products in my trunk for emergency purposes, because that shit right there was definitely an urgent situation. How would I have explained to Supreme why I smelled like some damn urine? Precious' egotistical ass was a pain even though she was on lock down. I was looking forward to the day I would lullaby that ass and have her out of all of our lives once and for all.

As I was relishing in my thoughts of ending Precious' life, my daydreaming came to a halt. I noticed one police car and what looked to be an unmarked car parked in the driveway as I drove past the gates.

"Damn, I wasn't expecting for Supreme to call in the cops so soon," I said, checking my appearance in the mirror. My once sleek jet black bob was now loaded with curls after the shower I took to kill all traces of the urine stench Precious left on me. My face was makeup free so I dabbled on some lip gloss to give a little life hoping to cover the worry lingering in my eyes.

I slowly made my way to the front door, answering in my mind every possible question that might be thrown my way. When I went to unlock the door I realized I had put my keys in my purse. I began rummaging through it and instantly noticed the pink diamond necklace I had yanked off of Precious' neck. Just then the front door opened and a familiar face was standing in front of me.

"Maya Owens, correct?" the pale white man with short spiked flaming red hair asked. When I zoomed in on his beady blue eyes I quickly remembered who he was.

"Yes, and you're Detective Moore. How are you?"

"I've been better, and I'm sure so have you."

"What do you mean?"

"I mean with your best friend missing and all."

"Precious, yes, but has it been determined that she's actually missing?"

"Do you think it can be something else?" he questioned with a raised eyebrow.

"I have to go to the bathroom really bad. Can you excuse me for one second?"

"Sure, I have to get something out of my car. I'll

be waiting in the living room for you when I get back. I have a few questions I need to run by you."

"No problem, I'll be right back." I ran upstairs with the swiftness. From the corner of my eye I noticed Supreme and another officer sitting in the living room talking. My heart was racing and I had to get away from Detective Moore. It was freaking me out that Precious' necklace was in my purse, and if he caught sight of it, the jig would be up. I ran in my room, tossed my purse on the bed, took a few deep breathes and headed back down the stairs ready for my interrogation.

"Is everything okay? You seemed to be in some sort of rush when you came in here," Supreme asked.

"Yeah, I had to go to the bathroom and didn't think I could hold it much longer. What's going on here? Did you find out anything about where Precious might be?"

"We're working on that. You suggested that maybe Precious wasn't missing. Do you have another scenario of what might've happened to her?" Detective Moore asked, walking up from behind me. I peeped a puzzled look on Supreme's face and I wanted to bitch slap Detective Moore.

"No, I don't have any other scenarios. I just didn't know that it had been decided she was missing."

"Then what could it be?" Detective Moore continued to press.

"I have no clue. Isn't that the job of a detective to figure things out? Isn't that why you're here?"

"Actually, we came to speak to Mrs. Mills about

another matter, and that's when Mr. Mills informed us that he didn't know where his wife was."

I glanced at Supreme, totally confused as to what was going on. Supreme put his head down and didn't say a word.

"What something else did you come to speak to Precious about?" I inquired.

"Remember when we were investigating the kidnapping of Aaliyah and the drive by shooting both you and Mrs. Mills were involved in?"

"Yes, I remember."

"Well, we told Mr. and Mrs. Mills that ballistics matched the unregistered gun used in the drive by with an unsolved murder in New York."

"Okay, and your point?"

"It's someone that's linked to another unsolved murder in the New York area that Mrs. Mills knew." Detective Moore looked down at a piece of paper obviously trying to pretend he didn't remember the name of the murder victim. "His name was Terrell Douglas."

"I don't recognize that name," I said, lying through my teeth. I would never forget Terrell.

"He lived in New York and was the younger brother of a Nina Douglas who was engaged to Mrs. Mill's childhood friend, Jamal Crawford."

"It's still not ringing a bell, sorry."

"Mrs. Mills was one of her bridesmaids and you actually accompanied her to the dress fitting at the bridal shop in Manhattan, correct?"

"Yes, now I remember," I said, casually. "So the same gun that was used in the drive by is the murder weapon used in the unsolved killing of Nina's brother. I never knew Nina had a brother, but then again, I didn't know her that well. What a crazy coincidence."

"That's the thing. I don't believe in coincidences. What are the chances that Terrell, who was related to Nina who was friends with Mrs. Mills, would both end up dead and neither of their murders has ever been solved? Then the same gun used to kill Terrell ends up in a drive by against you and Mrs. Mills. That doesn't seem like a coincidence to me."

"Wasn't Nina working for my brother?"

"From the information I gathered from the NYPD that seems to be the case."

"Then it kinda makes sense."

"What do you mean?"

"I'm saying Mike was behind the plot to kill Supreme and the kidnapping of Aaliyah and the drive by. Maybe he was responsible for both Nina's murder and her brother's too."

"You could very well be correct. I just find it strange that right when we're starting to make some headway on the case that Mrs. Mills disappears."

"Detective Moore, get the fuck out my house!" Supreme demanded, rising up off the white sofa, pointing towards the front door.

"Mr. Mills. you need to calm down."

"No, you need to shut the fuck up! My wife is missing and you want to come over here on some bullshit fishing expedition about some unsolved murder that happened in NYC. That ain't even your motherfucking jurisdiction."

"Mr. Mills, we are following all leads, and when that weapon ended up being used in a crime that took place in Los Angeles, the investigation did become part of our jurisdiction."

"My wife ain't killed nobody and she didn't just disappear. Some foul ass shit done happened. But just like I had to do things my own way to bring my daughter home, I'll do the same to get my wife back since you dumb fucks can't never seem to be able to solve shit."

"Taking the law into your own hands is never the way to seek justice. I promised you we'd bring your daughter home, and we delivered," Detective Moore bragged.

"You didn't deliver shit! If anybody deserves credit for bringing Aaliyah home it would have to be Maya, not the LAPD."

Detective Moore and his partner both turned towards me with a look of antipathy. Shit, I didn't care because I was beaming on the inside. Maybe working my powers of persuasion on Supreme wouldn't be as difficult as I thought.

"Mr. Mills, we should be going."

"Yes, we finally can agree on something."

"If you hear from your wife, please have her contact us. But we will do our own investigating, and if we find out anything I'll let you know."

"I'm sure you will. You know your way out."

Detective Moore and his partner took their time leaving, with their eyes slithering around as if they thought Precious was going to jump out from hiding.

Clueless that I had her chained up in a basement so far the fuck out that the location wouldn't even pop up on the top-of-the-line navigation system.

When the door finally slammed closed all I heard was a thunderous crash followed by a loud, "Fuck!" Supreme had thrown an antique marble vase across the room and it broke into a million pieces.

"Supreme, I know you're upset...so am I, but try to calm down."

"Maya, I don't want to hear it. Please, just go get Anna so she can clean up that shit. I don't want Aaliyah to see it."

"I understand. I'll go find Anna." After I looked in the kitchen and outside by the pool for Anna I decided to go upstairs thinking she was putting Aaliyah down for a nap. Throughout my search, the disgusting glare Detective Moore gave me kept replaying in my head. I knew he didn't like me and that was cool, but I was more afraid of him trying to link me to a criminal act. In subtle ways he made it clear that he felt something wasn't quite right with my self defense explanation after Clip and Destiny were killed. But without evidence to back up his suspicions he couldn't prove it. He had a hard-on for me since then, and that could lead to a lot of trouble.

When I got to Aaliyah's room the door was slightly ajar and I stuck my head in, but the only person I saw was Aaliyah lying in her crib. I went closer and observed her sleeping so peacefully. "Oh, she fell asleep with the bottle in her mouth." I picked up the bottle and rubbed her cheek. "You really are a beauty. Maybe one day soon your daddy and I can give you a little brother to play with since your mommy won't be able to do so." I bent over, kissed her forehead and then headed towards Anna's room, passing mine on the way, and noticed a figure by my bed. I tiptoed closer and through the crack of the door I saw that it was Anna. At first I thought she was cleaning my room and about to make up my bed, but then I realized what she was holding in her hand.

Oh fuck, the necklace! I told that nosey bitch to stay out of my room, but she's so damn hard headed. Calm down Maya. You've come too far to start fucking up now.

"Anna, I was looking for you. Mr. Mills wanted you clean up a little mess he made downstairs," I stated calmly.

"Miss Maya, you startled me!" Anna said, grabbing her chest as her body jumped.

"I'm sorry, I didn't mean to do that. What is that you're holding in your hand?"

Anna was so caught off guard she forgot she was holding not only my purse, but the necklace in her hand. "I was about to put some clean linens on your bed and your purse fell."

I did peep some fresh sheets on the dresser so I believed she was telling the truth, but the damage was done. "I told you there was no need for you to clean my room, that I would do it myself."

"I know, but it's a habit. Mrs. Mills always likes every room to be perfectly clean."

"But Mrs. Mills isn't here, I am. I also see that you're holding a necklace."

"Yes, yes, yes, it fell out your purse. This is Mrs. Mills' necklace. May I ask what you're doing with it? I'm only asking because she never takes it off."

"How true. But Precious asked me to hold it for her before she disappeared," I said, grabbing my purse and the necklace out of Anna's hand.

"I think I should go give this to Mr. Mills," Anna said, reaching her hand out, trying to take the necklace back.

"That's okay. You go clean up that mess and I'll bring the necklace downstairs to Mr. Mills myself."

Anna was reluctant to leave and kept eyeing the necklace. But when I didn't budge she made her exit. I waited a few seconds after Anna left the room and then I threw the necklace in the bottom drawer beneath my undergarments. I sprinted out my room. Anna was halfway down the hall and I was right on her tail. After she hit that first step, I used my right foot to kick her in the lower part of her legs. She completely lost her balance which sent her free-falling down the sweeping double staircase. Her eerie screams filled the air. I then placed Aaliyah's baby bottle on one of the top stairs so it would appear to be the cause of her unfortunate accident. If only she had minded her business, none of this would've happened.

When Anna's body finally hit the bottom, landing and I heard the loud thump, I stood watching for a few moments to see if there was any movement. Once I was pretty sure she was dead, I went back to my room and closed the door. Hell, I didn't want to be the one who discovered her body. When a crime is committed, it's better to have no clue...*clueless!*

Precious
Live Till I Die

The days were beginning to run together to me. I couldn't calculate how many hours had passed, what time it was or anything. But what I did know was that a bitch was hungrier than a motherfucker. Mike hadn't given me shit to eat since I got here. He reneged on that one day he mentioned feeding me, saying it was punishment for tossing my piss on Maya...what the fuck ever! All he had given me was tap water so I wouldn't become dehydrated and die. Then that bath Maya insisted I needed was a no go too. At this point I was tired of looking and smelling myself. My once pristine white pantsuit was turning into dirty gray. My mind and body were becoming weak and there wasn't shit I could do about it.

Right when I was about to doze off the light came on

and I heard the door opening. Then I heard the familiar sound of the stairs creaking as Mike came down.

"Good afternoon, Precious," Mike said as he stood over me.

I remained silent having no energy to respond. "Damn, babe, you look like a piece of shit. But I have good news. I feel that you've been punished long enough, and not only am I going to feed you but I'm going to let you bathe too."

Even with the encouraging news I was still mute.

"Precious, did you hear what I said?" Mike asked, lifting up my chin.

I nodded my head yes.

"I need for you to speak up. You need to show me some gratitude."

"Thank you," I muttered weakly.

"That's more like it. I'll be right back."

It seemed I had become numb to the pain in my stomach from not eating. But when Mike came back with a tray of food, I wanted to jump at it like a stray dog that had been eating out of trash cans for weeks. "Thank you, Mike. I mean that sincerely."

"I bet you do. It's amazing how starving an individual can bring out the best in them," he smiled. "Now do I have to feed you, or can I trust you'll behave if I take off the handcuffs?"

"I'll behave. I just want to eat." I meant that shit too. As much as I despised Mike, he was my savior at this particular moment. When those handcuffs came off I demolished the fried chicken, macaroni and cheese, greens and biscuit he prepared for me. I didn't know who cooked the meal but it was so damn good. But a can of Spam would've been good to me right about now.

"Slow down, Ma, the plate ain't going anywhere," Mike joked. But I kept on grubbing, licking fingers and all.

"I can't believe you're feeding me such good food, since you only promised me bread and water, and I had only received the latter so far."

"You got lucky. Devon brought over some lunch from this soul food restaurant and there was a lot left over. I was in a good mood and decided to share some with you."

By the time I finished eating the last chicken thigh I was completely full. Going hungry for however many days it had been made my heart ache to all the kids in the world who were truly going without. You never really have an understanding of that type of existence until you fuck around and find yourself in that predicament.

"I see you didn't leave not a crumb," Mike said, picking up my plate. "So are you ready to wash off that funk on you?"

"Been ready, but what am I going to put on? I mean there is no sense in me taking a bath if I'ma have to wear the same funky clothes."

"I got you covered."

"Oh...so why are you being so decent to me all of a sudden?"

"Real talk, you look so pathetic that I feel sorry for you," Mike laughed.

"Well, I'm glad one of us can laugh about my circumstances."

"You're right. There is no humor in this but it is what it is. There's nothing we can do."

"Yes there is. You can let me go home to my husband and daughter."

"Precious, I feel sorry for you, but I'm not stupid. You know that's not even a possibility."

"Why, because Maya says it's not?"

"No, because too much shit has happened."

"What are you getting out of this, Mike?"

"Revenge, what else?"

"Revenge on who, me? What did you expect? You tried to have my husband murdered and you raped me. There wasn't any other option. You had to go to jail, or die one. You know how the game goes. The police were already on to you, so don't blame me because you got locked up."

"Well since you know how the game go so well, then it shouldn't be no surprise to you that you're chained up in this motherfucking basement, now should it. So do you want to keep sitting here running off at the mouth or do you want to take a fucking shower before I change my mind?"

"I wanna clean my dirty ass, so I'll shut the fuck up."

"Good choice," Mike said, unlocking the chains around my legs. "Now I don't want no shit from you, Precious. If I think you're getting out of line, I'ma break your neck."

"I know. But I won't give you any problems. I'm just grateful to be having some hot water splash against my body." When I stood up, Mike held my arms behind my back firmly. "Is that really necessary? I mean for all that you shoulda kept the handcuffs on."

"Here you go again running off at the mouth."

"Okay, I'll be quiet, but please don't walk too fast. My legs are still a bit numb from sitting down for so long."

Mike led me up the stairs slowly, and when he opened the door it was as if we entered another world—make that another planet. No longer was I in the misery of a windowless, dreary basement. I had arrived in a mini mansion that was bananas! I had been in some fly cribs, but the architectural design was downright stunning. When I turned my head to the right, I could see the spacious entry with walls of glass that led to a floating glass and stainless steel staircase. When I turned to my left there was a massive wall of glass for an incredible 180° view. The shit was truly breathtaking. I couldn't comprehend that all this was going on up here and all that was going on down there, in what I considered a dungeon.

"Mike, I ain't tryna be funny, but who in the fuck do you know that let you stay in this crib, and do they have any idea you have a hostage chained up in the basement?"

"Funny, but this my shit."

"Yeah, right."

"What, you think Supreme the only one with long paper?"

"Umm, well you have been locked up, or have you forgotten that already."

"Nah, trust I definitely ain't forgot that shit. But like I told you a long time ago, I'm one of the few *real* kingpins. Niggas like me still be making major moves behind bars. That shit don't stop."

"I see," I said, doing a double-take of the ridiculously fly domain.

"Come on, let me take you to the bathroom you'll be using. I left your change of clothes on the table in there. The shit you have on needs to be burned, so you can drop them in the trash bag I put in there for you."

"Fuck you! This is a thirty-five hundred dollar Chloe pantsuit that you fucked up from having me locked up like an animal."

"Maybe now you know how it feels."

"Spare me," I said entering the bathroom.

"I'll be posted right outside this door so don't try no slick shit."

"Oh please! I know when I can't win and it's time to give up," I said closing the door behind me.

Damn, it seemed that everything in this house was made of glass including the bathroom, I thought as I peeled the filthy clothes off my back. I was more than happy to toss them into the plastic bag. Besides bathing products and the change of clothes, it seemed Mike had made sure all potential weapons were banished from the bathroom. Even if I wanted to make a move I didn't see anything that I could use.

I decided to enjoy the pleasure of a hot shower and be done with it. When the water hit my skin, it felt almost as good as an orgasm. It was like the water was making love to me and I welcomed it. In the midst of being seduced in the open shower, my eye caught what looked to be the rim of a trashcan. It was behind the toilet and almost unnoticeable. At the very moment I saw it, the next second my mind began plotting. I knew it was a stretch but I had to exercise all options because I knew they would be few and far between.

After showering for a few more minutes I walked away from the still running water and dried myself off. Then I went to the sink to brush my teeth and noticed the large mirror. I stood frozen, as I hadn't seen my own reflection in what seemed like forever. I touched my face gently and my cheeks had already begun to become sunken in. I had dark circles around my eyes from not getting any decent sleep. My normal bronzed butterscotch complexion appeared dull after being deprived of sunlight for so long. Now I could see why Mike felt sorry for me. I did look pathetic.

Once I took a few moments to feel sorry for myself it was time to get dressed. I was taken aback when I saw that my change of clothes was a cotton candy pink Juicy Couture jogging suit. It was my favorite loungewear, and on a few occasions when Mike had come to visit me I would have it on. I wondered if he remembered and that's why he left it for me. But I couldn't dwell on that as I was now on a mission.

I put my ear to the door to see if I could hear any movement or if Mike was guarding the bathroom like he said. I then bent down on my knees to see if I could get a peep of his shoes under the bottom opening of the door. I didn't see anything at first, but then I saw him walking across the hallway going into the living room I assumed. I stood up and grabbed the trashcan from behind the toilet. It was solid stainless steel, exactly what I needed to cause some damage.

I bent back down to once again place Mike's movements. This time I didn't see anything. I quietly cracked the door open and it was clear. I quickly slid out of the bathroom with the trashcan in tow. I closed the bathroom door and stood behind the hallway corner out of sight. My heart was thumping so hard I felt that all of LA could hear it. I heard some classical music coming from the living room area and presumed Mike was in there chilling, although I never figured him to be up on that style of tunes. But the soothing melody was surprisingly helping me to relax and my mind to focus a tad bit better. I had no idea how I was going to get the fuck out of this damn house.

As I pondered my next move I heard footsteps and they were coming in my direction. I leaned my back up against the wall and didn't even take a breath.

"Precious, you're still taking a shower?" Mike yelled, knocking on the bathroom door. I purposely kept the water running so he could think just that. I didn't have a watch on but it felt like I had been in the bathroom for thirty or forty minutes so I was sure by now he was wondering what the hell was taking me so long. Mike stood by the door for a few more minutes and then knocked again. "Something ain't right," I heard him say as he opened the door.

Fuck, it's now or never! I leaped around the corner and his back was to me as he stepped inside the bathroom.

"Precious, what the hell are you doing in here?"

As he asked the question out loud, I swung the trashcan up high. Mike must've felt my presence from behind because instead of me getting a clear landing on the back of his head, I caught the side of his face as he turned towards me. But the power of my blow did some damage because he stumbled and fell to the floor on his back. This was my one shot at freedom and I blew wind sprinting out the bathroom and down the hall. My legs were striding as if I was competing for an Olympic Gold Medal. There was no looking back to see who I leaving in the dust as it was winner take all, and that was gonna be me...or so I hoped.

As I continued to strive to reach my destination, it seemed like I was running down a never ending hallway. I knew that shit couldn't have been as long as it felt, but the closer I got to the front exit the further away it seemed to be. My mind was playing crazy tricks on me, so I just kept running.

At last I could taste freedom. I was right there. My hand reached out for the doorknob as I unlocked the top bolt, and then swung the door open. The sun instantly shined on me like it did for Ceily in the "Color Purple" as she ran through the field towards her sister who she hadn't seen in so long. But there would be no loving embrace between families like I saw in the movie. Instead, I felt a sharp excruciating pain and my last thought before I went unconscious was that I would try to live till I die.

Maya
Foolish Fool

"I still can't believe Anna's dead," Supreme said as he poured himself a glass of Remy Martin X111 cognac. "First my wife disappears, and now Anna is deceased, all within a week's period of time. I'm beginning to believe this house is cursed."

"Supreme, don't do this to yourself. What happened to Anna was a tragic accident."

"Tragic is right...to trip on a baby bottle. How unlucky can someone be? Can you imagine if she had been carrying Aaliyah?" That thought made Supreme pour himself some more Remy. "Damn, I need my wife right now!" Supreme continued taking down his cognac in one gulp.

"I haven't given up. I believe Precious will be back soon," I said, pretending to be optimistic.

"I hope you're right."

"I am."

"Maya, I know I've been harsh with you since Precious went missing and I'm sorry. Honestly, I don't know what I would've done without your support, especially for Aaliyah. You've been wonderful with her these last few days."

"It's nothing. You know how I feel about Aaliyah. I love her as if she was my own daughter," I said, cuddling Aaliyah as she bounced on my lap.

"It's so hard for me right now because every time I look at her I see Precious. My little angel is the only thing keeping me sane right now."

"Have you gotten any new leads on what happened to Precious?"

"Hell no! It's like she vanished into thin air. The surveillance tapes the cops confiscated showed nothing and the private investigators I hired can't come up with shit. I don't want to think it, but I have to wonder if once again Pretty Boy Mike is behind this."

"Sorry to interrupt, Mr. Mills, but the front gate called up and said that Detective Moore is here to see you."

"Thanks, Devon. You can send him in when he gets here."

"Were you expecting Detective Moore?" I asked as a feeling of anxiousness hit me.

"No, but maybe he has some news about Precious."

What the fuck is that fucking detective snooping around for this time? He ain't got no news. If anything, he's coming over here trying to dig up some news. That sonofabitch is about to work my very last nerve.

"Mr. Mills, Ms. Owens, nice to see you, although I wish it was under different circumstances. I heard about your nanny, Anna. It seems to be one tragedy after another in this family," Detective Moore commented as he took it upon himself to sit down.

"We're handling it. What brings you by here today?" Supreme put his glass down and folded his arms.

"Mr. Mills, I'm assuming still no word on your wife's whereabouts?"

"You're assuming correctly, but I hope you didn't come all the way over here to tell me something that I already know."

"Well, let's see. Did you know that your wife's cell phone records show that the last person she spoke to was Nico Carter?" I watched as the vein in Supreme's forehead pulsated and every muscle from his jaw down throbbed. "From what I understand, your wife and Nico Carter share a long history together."

"What's your point, detective?"

"I don't have a point…yet. Merely trying to connect the dots. But I have reached out to Mr. Carter. Unfortunately my office hasn't been able to get in touch with him yet."

"Are you saying you think he has something to do with my wife's disappearance?"

"Maybe, maybe not, but from what we've gathered so far he is the last person she spoke to on her cell phone. We're also looking into the possibility that Ms. Owens' brother, Mike could be behind this," Detective Moore said, turning his mug directly towards me. "Have you had any contact with your brother, Ms. Owens?"

"No I haven't. But with all the heat on him, I doubt he would take a chance and come back to LA."

"In my twenty years of detective work, I've learned you can never underestimate what a deranged, sick criminal is capable of, which includes your brother. He seemed to have a strong fixation on your wife." Detective Moore now turned back to Supreme. "Maybe he threw caution out the window and came back to finish the punishment on your family that he had started."

"I thought about that, but he would need resources, money, and with Clip dead I don't see how it's possible."

"Maybe he had more than just Clip and that young woman, Destiny helping him out. I mean somebody had to be behind the wheel of the car during that drive by, and I seriously doubt it was Mike. And who knows? It may also be the shooter from the unsolved murders of Terrell and Nina Douglas."

"Oh, so I guess that means you no longer suspect that Precious had any involvement with either one of those murders?" I inquired.

"I never said Mrs. Mills was a suspect."

"But you did imply that last time you came over, Detective Moore," Supreme reminded him.

"I simply wanted to ask your wife a few questions because I was made aware that at one time Mrs. Mills was friends with one of the victims."

"Precious doesn't have any friends besides me. Nina pretended to care about Precious because she was working for my brother."

"Right. Well again, this is all speculation. I'm gathering

as much information as possible in hopes that it will answer all of our unanswered questions," the detective said, standing up from the couch. "I'm sure I'll be in touch soon. But of course if either one of you come across any new information, give me a call."

"Will do, detective," Supreme said as he poured himself another drink.

"By the way Maya—is it okay for me to call you Maya?" Detective Moore asked, catching me off guard because he had practically reached the front door.

"Of course. It is my name," I smiled as I continued to hold Aaliyah.

"Do you recall seeing Nina Douglas on the day she was murdered?" he asked, walking back towards my direction.

"Uh, no I don't."

"I only ask because I know you were an invited guest to the wedding but never showed up."

"And who told you that?"

"I had an opportunity to speak with Jamal Crawford, Nina's fiancée at the time. He specifically remembered that you were supposed to come to the wedding with Precious but neither of you showed up."

"That's right, but, umm, it was so long ago. If I'm not mistaken, I was planning on attending the wedding with Precious but I had some boyfriend issues. Precious stayed with me to work them out and it ended up getting too late for us to make the wedding."

"And who was your boyfriend at the time? Would that have been Clip?"

"I don't believe so. I think it was another guy. But

what does any of this have to do with Nina's brother's murder?" I was about to end my statement with a four letter word but kept my tongue intact. I knew the sneaky detective was dying to get a reaction out of me but I wasn't about to give it to him.

"As I stated before, I have a hunch that the two murders are somehow connected. But I could be wrong. I would ask you for that boyfriend's name but I'm sure you've forgotten it by now," he remarked, not bothering to wait for my response. "Again, I must be going, but like I said, I will be in touch."

My blood was boiling as I watched Detective Moore finally stroll out of the door. "That man has a lot of nerve."

"Yeah, he does, but Maya, do you know anything about Nina's murder or her brother's?"

"Of course not."

"What about Precious? Did she ever mention anything to you about what happened to Nina?"

"No, but…" I cut my sentence off to give Supreme the impression I was holding something back.

"But what?"

"It doesn't matter. We need to be focusing on finding Precious not letting Detective Moore stir up trouble."

"Listen, Maya, if you know of Precious having any involvement in a murder let me know so I can do what's necessary to clean the shit up before it gets out of hand."

"I don't know anything specifically about Terrell, but after Nina was murdered Jamal came by the house to see her. He was vexed. He and Precious had a heated exchange of words. When he left, Precious said that she hoped he would let sleeping dogs lie when it came to finding Nina's killer. I did take it as if she was trying to protect herself."

"Did she say anything else?"

"No, and I didn't ask. If she was involved in Nina's murder I didn't want to know anything about it." I reflected back on that day I put a bullet in Nina's back trying to protect Precious. After that, I won her over because I proved my loyalty. It was the exact loyalty I needed Precious to believe I had in order to take her down.

"I understand," Supreme said, shaking the ice cubes in his glass. He seemed to be drifting off into some sort of trance. But I didn't believe it was so much the possibility that Precious might've killed Nina that had him stuck. Finding out that Nico was the last call Precious received, I felt, was the real reason he was in a daze.

"Supreme, it's so beautiful outside I thought it would be nice to take Aaliyah to the park, if you don't mind." He remained completely silent. "Supreme," I called out again snapping him out of his trance.

"I apologize. What did you say?"

"I wanted to take Aaliyah to the park, is that okay?"

"Sure, let me call one of my security guys so they can escort you."

"What about Devon? He's already here."

"That works. Here, take this," Supreme said pulling out a wad of cash.

"Supreme, no, I don't want your money."

"Take it. I want you and Aaliyah to enjoy yourselves."

Supreme gently rubbed Aaliyah's cheek and kissed her forehead. "Devon, just the person I wanted to see."

"What can I do for you, Mr. Mills?"

"Maya is taking Aaliyah out, so please escort her wherever she wants to go."

"Will do, sir."

"Bye baby. Daddy will see you later on. And Maya, thanks."

"I told you before; you don't have to thank me."

As I walked behind Devon while holding Aaliyah, I couldn't help but crack a smile. Supreme was vulnerable and emotionally close to the edge. All I needed to do was give him a little push so then I would be the only person he could turn to. When I got to the door, I turned around and waved goodbye to Supreme. It was crazy that a man whose presence was so strong and powerful was about to be putty in my hands.

After Devon opened the car door for me I buckled Aaliyah in her car seat and instantly got to yapping off at the mouth. "That fucking Detective Moore is making my stomach nauseated. That white prick needs to be shut the fuck down."

"Do you really have to use that language in front of the baby?" Devon questioned as he drove off.

"Shut the hell up! It's not like Aaliyah can understand what the fuck I'm saying. You just fucking drive."

Devon shook his head as if I was doing some sort of developmental damage to the baby.

"Anyway, like I was saying, Detective Moore, is a fucking problem."

"Why do you say that?"

"He's digging awfully deep into the murders of that Nina chick and her brother. But what I'm trying to understand is how Donnell ended up using the same gun in that drive by with me and Precious. Because that link right there is what is fucking all this shit up."

"Who gave Donnell the gun?"

"It wasn't me and I know it wasn't you, so that could only leave Mike. What is that nigga up to?" I mumbled under my breath.

"But even if Mike did give Donnell the gun, why you so pressed about that Nina girl and her brother?"

"Because I have both of their blood on my hands. Ain't that many coincidences in the world, that the same gun used to kill Terrell's ass was used in that drive by. Soon Detective Moore is going to put that shit together and realize that I'm the one who is my brother's keeper."

"Yeah, that detective is going to be a problem."

"Exactly! That's why I need you to handle that."

Devon, hit the brake and turned around to stare at me.

"Nigga, you can't stop the car in the middle of the street. You gonna cause a fucking accident."

"I know you not insinuating what I think you are!" Devon wanted to clear things up as he pressed back down on the gas.

"Yes the fuck I am."

"He's a fucking police officer! Have you lost your mind?"

"I don't give a fuck who he is. That motherfucka is about to mess shit up. Keep in mind, if he puts the pieces together, not only am I going down, but so are you." Devon frowned up his face, but that was real talk. That nigga couldn't think I would be doing a bid solo if shit hit the fan.

"I don't know, Maya. Killing a police officer…that's the death penalty."

"Shit, if Supreme finds out you were behind the kidnapping of his daughter and wife, you dead anyway. Plus, the only way you gonna get the death penalty is if you get caught—but you're not."

"How can you be so sure?"

"Because we're going to make sure the shit is tight. But the sooner we get rid of Detective Moore the better off we'll be. Now, we need to head over to the stash house so I can have a conversation with my brother. But before that, take me to the mall so I can spend some of this loot my future husband hit me off with."

"You think you have Supreme all figured out, don't you, Maya?"

"For your sake you better hope I do. With the devastation of him losing his precious wife, I need for him to become a complete foolish fool."

Precious
Player's Prayer

I struggled to open my eyes, but the throbbing from my head kept me closing my eyelids shut. I tried to reach my hand over and rub the pain piercing from the back of my head, but quickly realized they were handcuffed to some shit. The energy I used to shift my arms gave me the willpower to open my eyes the fuck up to see exactly where I was. At first, shit was looking real blurry as my eyes were half opened and half closed. But although my vision was playing tricks on me, my hearing was in top form, because even though I couldn't see them, I could clearly hear the conversation going on between Maya and Mike.

"Mike, why in the fuck do you have this bitch in the bedroom? Her ass is supposed to be chained up in the basement."

"Listen, let me handle Precious. You just tend to Supreme."

"Let you handle Precious? Dear brother, this is a joint venture. If anything, we handle shit together."

"Did you come all the way over here to drill me

about where I'm keeping Precious, or do you have something to say that's important?"

"As a matter of fact I do."

"Okay, then say it."

"Detective Moore has become a major problem. He's linked the gun that was used in Terrell's murder to the gun used in the drive by. And by the vacant stare on your face, you don't seem too surprised."

"I'm not."

"Then I guess you were the one who gave Donnell the gun."

"You guessed right."

"I thought you got rid of that gun a long time ago."

"It seems that I never got around to it."

"Why would you give that gun to Donnell to use in the drive by?"

"Insurance."

"Insurance on what?"

"You're a smart girl, Maya. Insurance on *you*. Just a minute ago you made the point that we're in this together, and you're right. With that gun being linked to both incidents, I've given Detective Moore enough ammunition to make you a suspect, but not enough to convict."

"Why would you do something so stupid?"

"Maya, you're my sister and I love you, but you can be rather impulsive. After you feel I'm no longer useful, you may get the stupid idea to hang me out to dry and claim that I was behind the kidnapping of Aaliyah, Precious and the murders of Clip, Destiny... oh yeah, and Donnell."

"I would never turn on you."

"I want to believe you and I hope you're telling me the truth, but in case you're not, like I said, I need some insurance."

"You ungrateful sonofabitch, I got you out of jail! You owe me!"

"And I've paid up. Look at you. You're living in the big house with Supreme, and I'm sure, plotting each day to go from houseguest to permanent bedmate. None of that would be possible without my help."

"We're blood, Mike? How can you treat me like your enemy?"

"If I was treating you like my enemy you would be dead. My beautiful little sister, if you play fair, you have nothing to worry about. You'll be able to live happily ever after with Supreme and I'll be able to live my life as a free man on an island somewhere. We'll both come out as winners."

"And what about Precious? When are you going to get rid of her?"

"Like I said, let me handle Precious."

"After all this time, you're still not over that bitch. Let it go, Mike, she'll never want you."

"Oh, you mean just like Supreme will never want you?"

"Speaking of Supreme, I'll be right back. I need to go to the car and check on Aaliyah."

"You left Aaliyah in the car? Are you crazy? It's hot out there!"

"Calm down! Devon is in the car and he has the A/C on. She was sleep when we got here and I want to make sure she didn't wake up."

"Let me find out your motherly instincts are kicking in."

"That little baby is the most valuable possession I'm working with. If I take excellent care of her, then Supreme will be all mine. I'm sure you've heard the saying, 'The hand that rocks the cradle rules the world."

"Indeed. Well I'ma go out there with you. I've missed seeing her face."

"Well don't get too attached. She's Supreme's daughter."

"Until we get that blood test, there is a very good chance she could be mines too!"

I heard the footsteps on the floor as Maya and Mike walked away. By this time my eyes were fully open and my lips were trembling from being so angry. The thought of my daughter being so close and not being able to see her, touch her, hold her, was about to make me insane. I also wanted to fucking know who this Terrell cat was and how was he connected to Maya. Being helpless was killing me.

Here I was, handcuffed to a steel framed canopy bed unable to move. The slick white, black and silver décor was much more appealing than the dreary basement I had been held captive in for weeks, but it didn't change my miserable circumstances. I then eyed the soaring ceiling and began recalling the last things I remembered before awakening to this room.

"Damn! I remember feeling *this* close to freedom, and then a sharp excruciating pain took me out cold. That must be where that throbbing on the back of my head came from. Mike hit the shit out of me with some sort of blunt object. But I wonder why he put me in this room instead of the basement?"

After going over my thoughts out loud, I then looked down at my clothes, and at first I was confused. I was expecting to see the dingy white outfit I had been wearing for what seemed to be forever, but instead I had on a fresh clean pink sweat suit and smelled of Glowing Touch body wash. "That's right, I did get to take a shower and wash my ass!"

So many things had changed since waking up from my mini coma and so many things had remained the fucking same. I could now take a sniff of my body without the odor making my stomach turn, but I was still a prisoner in this nightmare.

"I see you're awake," Mike said, entering the bedroom and startling me out of my thoughts.

"Barely. Whatever you hit me with really did a number on me. Do you mind telling me what it is you hit me with?"

"We can discuss that later. But listen. Maya's on her way back in here and don't mention that you tried to make an escape—we clear?"

"We're clear." Of course now my brain was in overdrive. Maybe what Maya said had some truth to it. Could Mike have unresolved feelings for me? If so, then I had to use that to my advantage. I detested that motherfucker, but now that I was back looking halfway decent it was time to exercise my female prowess on that nigga.

"Clear on what?" Maya said, sauntering her trifling ass pass her brother.

"I told Precious that because I now have her in the bedroom don't mean shit has changed."

"I don't understand why you put her up in here anyway. You need to take her ass back to the basement where she belongs, but I'ma leave that shit on you. Aaliyah is waiting for me, so I have to get done what I need and be the fuck out."

"Aaliyah is waiting for you where?" I asked, not wanting Maya to know that I overheard her conversation with Mike.

"She's in the car."

"Can I see her?"

"Bitch, you really have been locked up too long 'cause your ass delusional."

"It's not like she can go back and tell Supreme that she saw me."

"Precious, I'm not even entertaining your question. Here, I need for you to write something for me," Maya directed, completely brushing off my request.

"Write what?"

"A letter to your soon to be ex-husband."

"What type of letter?"

"Basically, that you've decided to leave him. You have some unresolved issues you need to work out and you don't know when or if you're coming back."

"You're fucking crazy! Supreme would never believe I would leave him, and especially my daughter."

"Look here. Detective Moore informed Supreme that the last person you spoke to on your cell was Nico. I had no idea Nico was such a sore spot for Supreme. Hell, maybe that'll be the unresolved issue you hint to in your letter."

"It'll never work."

"You better make it work. I don't give a damn what you think. Write this letter! And get it right the first time or not only will you be going back to the basement, but I'll also let my brother have his way with you," Maya said with a sinister chuckle.

"Maya, that's enough," Mike snarled, grabbing the paper and pen out of Maya's hand. "Precious, just write the letter so Maya can go."

I wanted to snatch the pen and stab both Maya and Mike in their eyeballs but thought it was time for me to start playing the game with Mike. "Fine, but can you take these handcuffs off of me so I can write it?"

Mike took the key out of his pocket and unlocked the cuffs. Maya stood smug faced, eating every second up. "Wait a minute, here's a clean piece of paper."

"What's wrong with the paper I already gave her?"

"Don't you see I'm wearing gloves? It's hot outside so it's not for weather purposes. When Supreme gets this letter, trust me, he and Detective Moore will have it tested for all fingerprint traces."

"You think you are so slick," I said.

"I learned from the best. Well, you *used* to be the best."

As I wrote the letter I knew Maya was probably damn near having an orgasm thinking she was that much closer to stealing my life. I wanted to shed a tear at the heartache I would cause Supreme when he read this bullshit, but wouldn't give Mike and Maya the pleasure of seeing my grief. When I was finished I put the pen down and Maya came over ready to run off, but read over several times what I wrote. Mike was right behind her securing my wrist with the handcuffs.

"This is perfect!" she said with a smile lighting up her face. "Oh, and I need for you to address this envelope also. Just in case you forgot, I wrote down your previous address, and at the top that's the sender address for you to use."

"You didn't forget shit, did you?" I said sarcastically.

"Just write." Maya stood over me making sure I dotted every 'i' and crossed every 't'. "As always, it was a pleasure seeing you, dear brother, but of course I must be going," Maya said, taking the envelope from my hand. "I know Supreme must be ready for me to come home and I don't want Aaliyah to wait any longer. With her mother gone and poor Anna deceased, me and her father is all she has."

"Anna is dead! What happened?"

"Oh, Precious. I'm so sorry but Anna had a tragic accident. It's such a shame. Poor thing tripped over Aaliyah's baby bottle and fell down the stairs."

"Would you please stop with that ridiculous, sarcastic sugary tone of yours? That was no accident! Your demonic ass killed Anna, but why?"

"If you must know, her nosey ass came across the necklace I ripped off your neck and she started drilling me. Then the silly fool said she wanted to give the necklace to Supreme...well you know I couldn't let that happen."

"It's never gonna stop with you. You'll kill anybody that gets in your way."

"True indeed! Gotta go!" Maya breezed out of the

room taking her dark cloud with her.

"Mike, I think you're scum, but I also know you're a very smart man."

"Your point?"

"The point is you know how this game works. Sooner or later you're going to be on that list of people who are in Maya's way. And the same way she had Clip taken out she'll do the same to you."

"I know how to handle my sister. She knows it won't be beneficial for her to cross me."

"Your sister is out of control. Don't you get it? She can't be handled! Soon you'll no longer be an asset to her, just a liability, and when that happens then it's lights out for you."

Mike wasn't saying shit but I knew the logic I was kicking was eating him up. From the conversation I overheard between him and Maya he had already come up with a backup plan in case Maya got outta pocket. So what I was spitting was only adding to his paranoia.

"Listen, Mike. I'm not tryna come between you and your sister. But after I'm dead I want to make sure that my daughter is safe. With Anna gone, there is no way Aaliyah will be safe with Maya. And although I never wanted to believe it, Aaliyah could very well be your daughter. Right now Maya is playing the sweet role because she needs Aaliyah to win over Supreme, but once that happens and she feels Aaliyah is in the way…need I say more? We both know what your sister is capable of."

Mike put his head down. He was trying to remain

calm but I could feel his anger building up. "Look, like I said, I'll handle Maya. And don't you worry about Aaliyah, she's straight. Now I have some things to take care of. I'll check up on you later."

When Mike got to the door he turned to me one last time before leaving. "That shit wasn't cool, tryna escape today, but then I wouldn't expect anything less from you," he said, before storming out.

I hoped that I pushed Mike's buttons enough to begin my process of divide and conquer. Maya was truly twisted, and being held captive gave me limited options so it would take all of my mental savvy to bring her down—that and a player's prayer.

I Run This

"Devon, I want to move on this Detective Moore situation immediately," I said, the moment I got in the backseat of the Bentley.

"What was Mike's opinion on how we should move?"

"I didn't ask for it, nor do I care too, and neither should you."

"But this is a team effort."

"Devon, *I* brought you in this team, not my brother. So you follow *my* orders. I don't want you discussing our plan for Detective Moore with Mike or anyone else."

"All I'm saying…"

"Fuck what you're saying!" I screamed, cutting Devon off. Aaliyah began wailing from the loudness of my voice. "It's okay, baby," I said, stroking her hair trying to soothe her.

"I told you to stop all that cursing in front of her. Now you've made Aaliyah upset."

"Save your parental guidance lecture. There would

be no need for me to curse if you would shut the fuck up and do what I say."

"You know what, Maya? I'm getting tired of you speaking to me like I'm some five dollar flunky," Devon growled, pounding his fist on the steering wheel.

I took a deep breath and changed up my approach since taking a hard line with him was defeating the cause. *What would Precious do under these circumstances?*

"Devon, I apologize for being so abrupt with you. I'm under a lot of pressure and I'm not only looking out for myself, but I'm looking out for you too."

"I can't tell."

"It's true. Do you think it was by accident that I went back to Brooklyn looking for you? That one older hustling cat I used to fuck with while I was dealing with Clip always spoke highly of you. He would preach to me that it was damn near impossible to find a loyal nigga, and that's why he made sure he always took care of you, so when I heard from one of my homegirls in BK that dude had got killed, I wanted to put you on."

"I feel you on that."

"I know how hard it is to maintain on them streets, plus you had family to take care of. I wanted to look out for you the way you looked out for him. But this the big leagues. When I recruited you I felt I made that clear. Mike is my brother and I love him. I'm grateful that you put me on to your man and we were able to get Mike out. I'm grateful for all the loyalty you've shown me and I plan on not only telling you but showing you too," I said, licking my lips seductively.

"I was under the impression you only had eyes for Supreme."

"Yeah, Supreme got all the coins and I need that to not only take care of me and my brother, but to also keep your pockets fat. But that don't mean a sexy nigga like you don't get my pussy wet. You feel me?" I was lying my ass off, but I needed this cat to do some serious dirty work for me. Supreme represented much more than an endless cash flow. I had been dying to suck his dick since I first saw him in a music video before I had even hit adolescence. Becoming his wife would give me bragging rights 'til the day I died.

"I fo' sho' feel you, Maya. You got my third leg excited over here. So when you plan on showing me how grateful you are?"

"Business first, and then pleasure."

"I guess that means we need to handle this Detective Moore problem as soon as possible."

"Now we're on the same page. But, umm, while you're mulling over when, where and how you're going to eliminate the detective, take me to the post office. I have a letter that needs to be mailed out."

When we pulled up to the post office I took out my book of stamps and peeled one off. I scanned the envelope again before placing it firmly on the upper right-hand corner. I dropped it in the mailbox, and a surge of newfound power shot through me. "Okay Devon, let's go home."

"Devon, remember, don't discuss our plans for

Detective Moore with anyone. Tomorrow at twelve o'clock I'll meet you at our spot so we can graph this shit out, so don't be late. I know you're working the three o'clock shift so promptness is a must."

"I got you. I'll be there."

"Good, now open the door for me. Our relationship has to appear strictly professional. You never know who's watching," I said, looking towards the front entrance of the house from the parked car.

"Whatever you say."

"While you're at it, carry in these bags for me," I directed as I took Aaliyah out of her car seat and headed inside. When I entered, Supreme was still in the same location as before I left. But instead of standing, he was slouched down in a chair with a drink in his hand.

"Where do you want me to put your bags?" Devon asked, interrupting my stare down of Supreme. Supreme lifted his eyes in my direction as if he only then realized we had come home.

"You can leave them right there," I said, pointing to the bottom of the wraparound stairs.

Devon put the bags down and then tried to linger his tired ass at the spot to further inspect what was about to go down between me and his boss.

"Thanks, Devon, you can go now." My stiff smile screamed get to steppin'!

Devon got the hint and nodded his head. "Mr. Mills, can I be of any further assistance to you this evening?"

Supreme appeared dazed for a minute and then he silently shook his head no. But that nigga wasn't dazed, he was drunk.

I was ready to push Devon's slow dragging ass out the fucking door. He was holding up my flow. He took his time getting the fuck out and kept glaring back after each step. When he finally bounced I virtually skipped to the door and locked it, making sure he couldn't make a sudden return. I didn't say shit to Supreme. I let him continue to drown his sorrow in that thousand dollar a shot Remy Martin and grabbed my bags and headed upstairs to Aaliyah's bedroom.

"Now, I need for you to be a good little baby and play in your crib until you fall asleep," I uttered to Aaliyah as I took off her clothes and put on her nightie. "I have to go work on your daddy, and I don't need no interruptions, so I'll see you in the morning." I kissed Aaliyah on her forehead, sat her in the crib, turned on the nightlight and made my exit.

As I dashed down the hallway, I made a pit stop at a mirror hanging in the center of the wall. I scrutinized myself and my appearance was definitely not on point. I had a long day and it showed. I wanted to take a shower and freshen up but didn't want to lose any momentum toying with Supreme. I hoped that although I was in semi-form, his drunken eyes would see dime piece. I took my chances continuing my dash downstairs and opening a few buttons on my blouse, along the way.

"Is everything okay Supreme?" I asked softly, watching him pour himself another drink.

"As good as shit can get for a nigga when your

wife been ghost for a couple of weeks and your daughter ain't got her mother," Supreme slurred.

"I know it's tough, but you have to be strong for Aaliyah."

"Yeah, but who gon' be strong for me?" he asked, plopping down on the couch spilling some of his drink.

"I will. I'll help you through this." I sat down beside him and rested my hand on his thigh without being too aggressive.

"Well then help me understand why my wife has been keeping in contact with the motherfucker that tried to kill her."

"You mean Nico."

"Motherfuckin' right I mean Nico!" he roared before greedily gulping down his drink in one hit.

"I think that's something you should discuss with Precious."

"I would if I could find her. Man, I shoulda had that nigga killed when I had the chance," Supreme babbled, caught up in his own world. "I ain't neva told Precious that I know this shit, but she fucked that nigga during the time she thought I was dead."

"How do you know that?" My ears perked up waiting as Supreme was revealing some new info that I knew absolutely nothing about.

"Man, towards the end of their investigation on Mike, the feds had a wiretap on Precious' cell. They wanted to see if he would make any incriminating statements to her over the phone so their case could be even stronger. I didn't find out until months later after they reviewed all the recordings what had went down between her and Nico."

"Who told you?"

"One of the agents I had got extra cool with when they had me in protective custody felt I had the right to know. He heard a few of the conversations between Precious and Nico and it was evident them motherfuckers shared a goodbye fuck. I promised I would never say shit because he could lose his job behind that bullshit."

"And you never confronted Precious about it?"

"When I found out I wanted to beat the shit out of her, but she was pregnant and of course I couldn't hurt our baby..." the word "baby" faded out from Supreme's mouth. "To this day Precious is clueless about that shit, and you need to stop frontin' like you didn't know what had went down."

"I swear I didn't, Supreme."

"That's supposed to be yo' girl and she ain't neva told you about it...but then again Precious is the secretive type. She don't trust nobody."

"I guess you're right because I damn sure didn't know. I feel bad that you've been carrying this around for so long. It's gotta be painful."

"It was. The only thing that made it a little easier to cope with was that when it happened, she did believe I was dead. Sometimes people turn to a familiar face for comfort when they hurtin'. Fuck, I don't know, because how can you go back and fuck a man that put a bullet through your chest? It makes me wonder if their connection is that strong," Supreme said, trying to stand up but quickly losing his balance and having to sit right back down.

"Supreme, I think you've had too much to drink." I leaned over brushing my breast against his chest as I took the glass from his hand.

"I'm straight. But I do need to go to bed. Dealing with that detective telling me that the last person my missing wife spoke to was a nigga I detest just as much as Pretty Boy Mike completely exhausted me."

"Let me take care of you. I'll put you to bed," I said, gently stroking the side of Supreme's face and rubbed my fingers through his low haircut. I got up and walked over to the bar and put down the glass and came back to the couch feinding to finish my seduction on Supreme, but his eyelids were closed shut and he was knocked out.

"Supreme, wake up...wake up!" I started shaking him but Supreme was out cold. Damn, my fuckin' luck! I was *this* close to riding that nigga's dick like a stallion and he want to pass out in a drunken stupor. I was so pissed I didn't even get him a blanket. I left his ass right there on the couch and I went upstairs to bed.

I was awakened early the next morning by the wet Pamper and I'm hungry screams of Aaliyah. I put the pillow over my head determined to kill the sounds echoing through the mansion. "Damn, babies are loud as hell," was all I could keep saying. That shit remained persistent for the next ten minutes.

"Anna, go get Aaliyah!" I screamed out, but then became conscious of the fact that Anna had died like a week ago. That was the first time I slightly regretted taking her nosey ass out. "Fuck!" I belted. I was used to Supreme caring after Aaliyah in the morning but he was probably still laid out on the couch from drinking himself to sleep.

I finally found the strength to drag myself out of bed, madder than a motherfucker. When I got to Aaliyah's room her nose was running, snot coming out from crying so damn hard. and babbling "Daddy" and "baba" for a bottle. She was pulling at her nightie, and when I got closer I saw it was soaking wet. Her urine-drenched Pamper was halfway off and it had saturated her nightgown.

This shit is for the fuckin' birds! This is what you have to go through as a mother. Getting no damn sleep, changing dirty Pampers, feeding a motherfucker and having to jump every time they start wailing. I don't know how much more of this shit I can take, especially since I ain't getting no dick!

I kept praying that at any moment Supreme would stride up in here and tell me he would handle this and I could go back to bed. But as the time slowly passed he was still a no show. It took almost thirty minutes for me to get Aaliyah cleaned up, take off the dirty sheets and tidy shit up.

With Aaliyah locked on my hip we took it downstairs so I could feed her. By this point I was tired of her sucking on her pacifier as if breast milk was spilling out. When we passed the living room Supreme was exactly like I left him and all I could do was roll my eyes, while Aaliyah started reaching out and once again calling out for her daddy. Not once did she call for her mommy so that let me know that she didn't have me confused with her mother. I didn't know whether to be mad or happy.

By the time we reached the kitchen, Aaliyah threw her pacifier on the floor and pointed towards the HDTV Sub-Zero refrigerator freezer. "Can't nobody ever say that you ain't got your mother's temper," I commented, grabbing a bottle from the fridge.

Aaliyah seemed to be ignoring me as she clapped her hands at the LCD TV DVD hookup with radio. I couldn't believe how far technology had come and what money could buy you. Who would've guessed that a piece of appliance that at one time was strictly to keep your food cold now included a top-of-the-line entertainment center.

"Yeah, I could most def' get used to this style of living." While I warmed up the bottle and began daydreaming of my life as the rich and fabulous, I heard the doorbell ringing. I glanced at the clock on the microwave and it was barely after nine o'clock.

"Who the fuck could this be?" I said, picking up the bottle with Aaliyah in tow. She yanked that bottle out my hand and latched onto the nibble as if starving. "What in the hell is he doing here?" I huffed, looking out the peephole.

"Good morning, Maya," Detective Moore greeted me as if we were friends. "What an adorable little girl," he said, doing some silly ass shit with his fingers towards Aaliyah. "I see you're making yourself right at home, Maya. I wonder what you'll do when the Mrs. comes back."

"What do you want, Detective Moore?" I ignored

his slick underhanded comment because again I knew he was trying to get a rise out of me.

"I came to speak with Mr. Mills. I have some new developments that I wanted to share with him."

"Supreme is sleep."

"I thought a successful businessman like himself would be up by now."

"He had a rough night. But you're more than welcome to tell me what your new developments are and I'll be happy to pass it along when he wakes up."

"No, I rather talk to Mr. Mills personally. I'll stop by later on either this afternoon or evening."

"Which one is it, afternoon or evening?"

"I don't know," he said, in a self-satisfied tone. I was now a hundred percent sure that this pompous sonofabitch was fucking with me. "I guess you'll know the answer to that when I pop back up."

"Suit yourself," I said, shutting the door in his face. I stood in the entry and then leaned my back against the wall. I had to bring an end to whatever the pesky detective was conjuring up once and for all.

****

"You're late!" were the first words that left Devon's lips when I sat down at the table in the quaint restaurant on Robertson Boulevard.

"I know this, but it took forever for Supreme to wake up and I wasn't about to bring Aaliyah with me."

"Wake up...what had him in such a deep sleep...

did you and him?"

"No. Your boss was too drunk to do anything or anybody. He passed out on the couch and didn't wake up until after eleven. It was torture trying to take a shower and get dressed with a baby up under me. Now I understand why every rich bitch has a fuckin' nanny. Boy, chicks in the 'hood would appreciate that shit. I think it's time for Supreme to start taking applications to fill Anna's position."

"Do you think that's wise with all the shit we have jumping off right now? I mean I would hate for another nanny to end up at the bottom of the stairs because they started asking one too many questions."

"You have a valid point, but damn, I don't know how much longer I can play this mother role."

"If you plan on being Mrs. Supreme Mills you better get used to it fast. That baby comes with the package."

"You don't have to remind me. I'm well aware of that fact. But enough about babies and shit. We need to address what this meeting is really about. Man, I've had enough of our little friend. Do you know he showed up at the crib this morning?"

"For what?"

"My take, he's fuckin' wit' me. But he claims he has some new information to share with Supreme and that still spells fuckin' wit' me."

"Did he say what the new information was?"

"I asked, but of course his answer was that he wanted to personally speak with Supreme. Thank goodness Supreme was sleep because in a perfect world the detective will never get the opportunity to say another word to him."

"I take it you want to move on this immediately?"

"Is 'like yesterday' soon enough?"

"I came up with a scenario that should work." Devon moved in closer and put his elbows on the center of the square wooden table. "I did some research with a few of my sources."

"Oh fuck! I told your stupid ass not to tell anybody what we were up to."

"Yo, calm down," Devon whispered, pulling my upper body towards him. "I didn't tell nobody shit. I have ways of getting information without arousing suspicion."

"You better," I warned.

"Listen, I'm putting my livelihood on the line. Do you really think I'ma do or say something to put me in jeopardy?"

"I feel you...go head, finish what you were saying."

"Well, I got our little friend's address, and I'm thinking a home invasion gone wrong would be the best look. Anything else will make it appear as if he was a target. But attempted robbery...shit, with the economy being so fucked up they running up in cribs first and taking names later."

I sat back taking in what Devon said. An attempted home invasion might be the strategy to run with. That would lead the investigation towards robbery instead of who might have a grudge against the relentless detective. Anything else probably would have officers prying into his open cases and leading them in my face for a million and one questions. "I think it could work.

So are you going to actually go in his crib or what?"

Devon pulled me back in and I wanted to puke because dude's breath smelled real tart. I wanted to give him a Tic Tac, Big Red or something but figured we had to take one thing at a time, and wiping out the detective was top priority.

"I'm looking to get him right outside his front door. On the low, I scoped out his house. He lives off a main street so that's a good thing because mad cars be coming through. He also has a lot of high bushes surrounding the entrance. I figure I can sneak up behind him and put a bullet through the back of his head and be out."

"I like the sound of that, Devon. So when is all this going down?"

"I'm leaning towards tonight. Detectives normally work late shifts so I was gonna head over there after I got off of work, but if I'm too late then tomorrow night. I'm off tomorrow so I'll have time to chill in the cut and wait him out."

"Damn, that means he'll have time to speak with Supreme today."

"Maya, you can't expect for me to do him in broad daylight. It's gotta be at night. Keep Supreme busy. Get him out the house so the detective can't talk to him. You're resourceful. I'm sure you can come up with something to keep Supreme occupied."

"Yeah, I'll suggest we take Aaliyah out for some ice cream or some child friendly bullshit. Try your hardest to make it happen tonight though. I don't think I can keep him away from Supreme for two days in a row. He's pretty fuckin' persistent, which is why he has to go."

"Then tonight it is. When you wake up tomorrow the detective will no longer be our problem, and then of course we'll have some celebrating to do."

"No doubt. I'm looking forward to it."

"Me too. A conniving bitch like you got to have some good pussy and I can't wait to be all up in it."

I simply grinned at Devon's remark. If his desire to take a dip in my juices would speed this murder up then I was willing to give him a taste right now. At this stage in the game anything was doable as long as Devon understood that this is my show and I run this.

Precious
Role Play

Being locked the fuck up will definitely humble a bitch. That's all I could think about when I woke up the next morning with my stomach growling. It was hitting me harder and harder each day that I went from chilling in a luxurious estate to being someone's prisoner, unable to have control over my next move.

After my slick antics with Mike yesterday he didn't show his face for the rest of the night. I yelled out a few times because not only was I starving, but had to piss. After wearing out my pipes for over an hour off and on, I finally accepted the fact the nigga wasn't fucking with me. I eventually fell asleep, pissy, hungry and now waking up to the same shit. As my eyes darted around the room trying to entertain myself I glanced down at my feet and got fixated on my chipped French pedicure, "Damn, I fell off!" was all I kept repeating until I heard the bedroom door being unlocked.

"I see your up," Mike said as if he didn't have a care in the fucking world. But why shouldn't he? It was obvious this nigga hadn't missed a meal or a grooming.

"I know you heard me last night screaming my ass off in here. Even prisoners get a bathroom break," I said, sucking my teeth.

"In this prison, using the bathroom is a privilege which you lost after trying to make your great escape."

"Oh, so what, you gon' have me pissing on myself for the duration of my stay?"

"Hopefully you've learned your lesson and it won't come to that, but we shall see." Mike came towards me and began unlocking my handcuffs.

"What are you about to do to me?"

"You wanna take yo' ass to the bathroom don't you?" That was one question that didn't even need a response. "Now come on, but I'm telling you now, I ain't in the mood for no bullshit this morning."

"I won't give you any."

"Aight, let's go."

It wasn't until I was in an upright position that Mike took a gun from his back pocket and held it to my spine.

"Is the gun really necessary?" I smacked.

"I learned my lesson dealing wit' yo' crazy ass, and for your sake I hope you did too."

When we entered the hallway the smell of breakfast food smacked me in the face. My stomach immediately started grumbling and I was tempted to start begging Mike for some food, but thought I needed to take one objective at a time. When we got to the bathroom I stepped in the entrance and started closing the door so I could handle my business on the toilet.

"Nah, you leaving the door open, shorty," Mike said, pushing the door back open.

"What the fuck, you got a gun patrolling my every move. Can't I at least do what I got to do in private?"

"No, you lost all rights to privacy. Now hurry up."

"I shouldn't have to share this wit' you but I need to shit."

"Go head, just make sure you spray that Oust afterwards and turn on the fan."

"That's how this is going down? I have to shit with the door open and you posted at the door?"

"Exactly. Now hurry the fuck up before I start making yo' ass wear diapers for now on."

"Fine, but could you at least turn around so I can maintain a little bit of my dignity?" Mike obliged my request but I still felt like less that zero grunting and shitting in front of this motherfucker. I knew I had done some foul shit in my life but this punishment right here was almost too much to endure. By the time I finished and wiped my ass all my pride had damn near diminished. I went to the sink and washed my hands, feeling defeated.

"Come on, it don't take that long to wash your hands, and don't forget to spray 'cause you stunk up the joint for real."

Once again as we began what I call the prison walk back to the bedroom, the smell of the food lingering in the air had my stomach sounding like a disgruntled tiger.

"What the fuck you stopping for?" Mike pushed the gun firmly in my back as I suddenly stopped a few feet away from our destination.

"Mike, I'm so damn hungry! Can I please have something to eat?"

This nigga didn't say shit. He stayed quiet and I imagined his trifling ass laughing behind my back.

"Don't make me beg, but I will," I said, not giving a fuck. What in the hell did I have left to lose? This nigga already had me shitting in front of him. We had come to the point where anything goes.

"I don't know. Last time I demonstrated some kindness and fed you, the favor was returned by you getting all this strength up to clobber me with a fuckin' trashcan and tryna break out. Food seems to be to you what spinach was to Popeye."

"Mike, I'm being serious right now."

"Shit, I'm serious too. Ain't nobody playing. The reason I didn't fuck wit' you none last night was because I was zoned out on medicine tryna get rid of the migraine you left me with. I ain't up with playing those types of games with you today."

"If you feed me I promise I'll be on my A game. I won't try no bullshit. I give you my word on that."

Mike came from behind and stood in front of me staring into my eyes intensely. I wanted to spit in his face and rip my claws through his skin, but instead I conjured up some big crocodile tears, enough to water up my eyes real good but not let a single one trickle down my cheeks. This would give a more convincing performance. Because everybody knows I don't shed a tear over shit, so this would give the appearance of me being on the verge of breaking down but trying to remain strong. Honestly, that wasn't far from the truth, but I'm a soldier. I don't lay down, I gets down, and slowly I was implementing my plan.

"Yo, are you about to cry?" Mike had a perplexed look on his face, stunned by my crushed expression.

I tilted my head down as if trying to hide my embarrassment of admitting defeat. "No, I'm good. Everything's cool," I said, clearing my throat.

Mike lifted my chin gazing in my eyes like this was some fucking love story. *Negro please!* was all I could think to myself. "No, you're not cool. I see this situation is finally taking its toll on you. I wondered how long you could remain tough, but even you have your breaking point, Precious."

"I said I was good, Mike. You can stop pretending like you give a fuck if I'm okay or not. I know you don't give a damn how I feel."

"That's not true. I do care about how you feel."

"I can't tell. You've tried to humiliate me every chance you got."

"I only wanted to humble you. Since the first time I met you, you've always had this mentality that the sun rises and sets on Precious' ass. I needed for you to understand that it doesn't."

"Your point has been made," I said, clapping my hands as if giving a mock standing ovation.

"Precious, stop! I'm kicking real shit right. From me kidnapping you and having you hauled up in here has always been about teaching you a lesson. You've always farted around like you was Miss Untouchable. I needed to show you that you're not. At this moment was the very first time that I've seen that you know that you aren't."

I wanted to burst out laughing that this slimy motherfucker who raped me had the audacity to stand in my face and give me a sermon on teaching someone a fucking lesson on humility. But, hell I was willing to play this bullshit out for this self righteous snake.

"I can't front. I don't like to admit I'm wrong about shit, but what you're saying is valid, I'll admit that."

"Wow, progress has finally been made." This nigga stood grinning real proud, as if he was being honored at some prestigious award ceremony. This clown was carrying on like I was some charity case that he reformed.

"Who would've thought that you, Mike could be the one to make me admit to my flaws. Once again, I've underestimated how much influence you have over me when I let my guard down."

Mike didn't respond verbally to what I said. Instead he grabbed my arms and led me into the bedroom and handcuffed me back to the bed. He left the room, still silent, closing the door behind him.

Oh fuck! Did I take that kissing ass shit too far? I thought I really had my performance tight and he was licking that shit up like a lollipop. Damn, right when I finally felt I was making a breakthrough with that sociopath I play my cards all wrong.

I kept shaking my head trying to figure out at what point did the conversation go wrong. I was dissecting each word that was exchanged between us so hard that at first I didn't hear Mike come back in.

"Sorry I took so long but the food was getting cold so

I had to warm it back up," he said, as he placed a tray of food on the dresser.

I was grinning so damn hard inside. I'm still that *bitch!*

"That's okay, I'm just so thankful you decided to bring me some food. You have no idea what you've just shown me." *That fucking a nigga will let you have him for one night, but stroking a nigga's ego will let you have his mind for a lifetime.*

"Yes, I do. That I'm genuinely concerned about what happens to you," Mike said, un-cuffing my hands.

"Exactly," I said, reaching for the tray of food. This dude had prepared a bacon and cheese omelet with grits and buttered crescent rolls. Then he had me washing my meal down with freshly squeezed orange juice.

"Precious, if you continue to cooperate with me your stay here can be a pleasant one." Mike was now eyeing me the same way I did my plate of food before quickly devouring it down.

"I don't see how any stay can be pleasant when you know eventually you're going to die."

"Plans can change. This doesn't have to end with you dying."

"So you say, but I don't think Maya is going for that."

"I told you before, let me handle Maya. All you need to focus on is being loyal."

"Loyal to you?"

"Of course."

"What I was trying to say was I'm surprised you want my loyalty because it's not like you need it," I said, trying to smooth over how appalling his request sounded to me.

"I do need it."

"Why?"

"Because if I let you stay alive I would need to know you would never cross me."

Boy oh boy, Mike surely had game with him. It took me a second, but I now understood what was going on in dude's head. He definitely was scheming to maneuver some pussy out of me, but see, the thing was he didn't want to have to take it like he did last time. This demonic fuck wanted me to spread my legs willingly!

"I understand the whole loyalty thing, but I can't lie and say that I don't have trust issues. A lot of foul shit has happened between us and it's hard to be loyal to someone that you don't know will be loyal back to you."

"That's real, Precious. That's why I'm making an effort to show you. I know I only have a little bit of time to prove that, but if you let me, I will."

"Why do you say that you only have a little bit of time?"

"Because within the next week I'll have my money and will be able to get out of LA and start a new life, hopefully with you."

I almost choked on my orange juice when Mike used the words "new life" and "with you" in the same sentence. "You want me to come with you?"

"You and Aaliyah. For the short period of time I spent with her it was as if we bonded. I can't help but believe she really is my daughter. Of course this is all contingent on you proving your loyalty," Mike quickly added.

"I woke up this morning ready to die and now you've given me a reason to live. How ironic is that shit?"

"It's a lot to swallow but I think it could work. From

the moment I laid eyes on you in the club a few years ago, I knew you had all the makings to be my wife. That shit ain't changed."

"The thought of being with Aaliyah again, this all sounds so promising, but I can't see Maya going for it. I don't think you understand how ruthless she is. You look at her as your baby sister, but trust me, Maya is no longer a little girl."

"You think I don't know that? I hardly recognize her anymore. But I try to be patient with Maya because I know a lot of it is my fault."

"Why do you feel like that?"

"Maya never knew her father and it affected her emotionally," Mike revealed with regret in his voice.

"I can relate to that. I still don't know who my father is."

"Neither does Maya. Even though my dad disappeared from our lives before Maya was born, she always believed we had the same mother and father, but we don't. I don't know who Maya's father is. My mother never told me and I didn't bother or care to ask. I figured he was another low life, like the rest of the men that came in and out of our lives. So Maya turned to me to be that father figure and I let her down."

"How?"

"I didn't protect her from the sorry ass men my mother would have up in her crib. I mean I don't believe none of them messed with Maya physically, but psychologically she always felt unwanted, as if our moms was choosing being with the men over her."

"Damn, I feel like I'm reliving my childhood all over again."

"The difference is Maya had me and I should've stepped up to the plate and been there for her, but I was too busy doing me. I was in those streets building a drug empire not understanding or caring that I was simply throwing money her way so she could stay out my face and let me do what the fuck I wanted to do. Now look at her. She's a killer just like her brother."

"Mike, you didn't make her into a killer."

"You don't have to spare no punches wit' me, Precious. Maya has no soul. The only reason you got yours back is because you fell in love and had a baby. The same would have to happen to Maya if she has any chance at redemption."

I swallowed hard, agonizing over what Mike said. This nigga was treacherous but he knew his shit. That is what saved me, and it was killing me inside that Maya was turning to Supreme to do the same for her. The difference was the love Supreme and I share is as real as it comes. It was no manufactured concocted bullshit. I was praying that he would remain loyal to our vows and commitment and not fall for the poison Maya was feeding him. But once he read the fake ass letter Maya had me write, I knew there was a strong chance all that dedication was history.

"Mike, I'm going to ask you a question and I want you to be honest with me."

"Go head."

"You're hoping that Maya will be able to make Supreme fall in love with her, aren't you?"

"Yes, but it isn't because I want to hurt you," he answered, taking my hand as if to appease me. I wanted to commence to whooping Mike's ass right there on the spot but kept telling myself to play the game or I would never see my family again. "But because when I leave I know she won't have anybody else. Maya needs Supreme, and with you gone he's going to need her too."

"Supreme deserves better than Maya, and so does my daughter."

"I feel you, and that's why Aaliyah will come with us. As for Supreme, you know I ain't checkin' for that cat, but if he can make Maya feel love and bring her some happiness then I'll let him be. Maybe this can right the wrong from her childhood and take away my guilt. Because no matter what, she's my blood and I love her."

"Mike, this is too much for me to deal with all at once. You're willing to strip away my life and hand it over to your conniving sister. She's got you feeling so guilty about the past that you ain't grasping how vicious she is. This ain't no Little Bo Peep has lost her sheep nursery rhyme shit. Your sister has some serious issues."

"There are some magazines in the drawer. Sit back, read them and relax," Mike said, standing up from the bed, obviously not wanting to face the harsh reality of who his sister truly is.

"What about the handcuffs?"

"I told you I was working on gaining your trust. This is a start. I will be locking the door but having the freedom to walk around the room will hopefully make you feel less like a prisoner and more of a welcomed guest."

"Wow, the surprises keep on coming! I certainly

wasn't expecting this, but again, thank you."

"I'm making an effort so I need you to do the same thing."

"Meaning?"

"Give what I requested of you a chance."

"You're talking about the loyalty thing."

"Yes. Or have you already made your mind up that it ain't gon' happen?"

"If it could mean being reunited with my daughter, then I'm willing to try."

"I always knew you were a smart woman, and the love you have for your daughter makes you even that more appealing. I'll be back later on to bring you lunch. Bye."

I stood up and then sat right back down wondering what the fuck had just happened. Could this nigga be serious or was this another sick game he was playing to further torture me? The vibe was clear that the attraction he had for me was very much intact, but wanting to fuck me and having us run off together with Aaliyah was two totally different things. Mike was a slickster in every sense of the word, but until I figured out what he was truly up to I would continue my role play.

Maya
From Nothin' to Somethin'

I rose up from my queen-sized bed feeling exactly like that…a queen. Today felt like a new beginning because if all had gone as planned, Detective Moore should be somewhere in the coroners office. I was tempted to call Devon to get the full report but opted against it, especially after that disclosure from Supreme about the feds putting a wiretap on Precious' cell phone. There was too much at stake to blow it all on a fucking phone call. Today was Devon's day off so I would have to wait for him to make contact.

I flipped on the television switch and turned to the news to see if there was any coverage about Detective Moore's murder. I twiddled my thumbs for over fifteen minutes watching everything from the weather report, entertainment news covering

Paris Hilton's latest sexual exploit, and local to international news, but nothing on a shooting death of a cop. I stared at the bottom of the screen for a breaking news alert but still nothing.

"Fuck it! Maybe his body is still sprawled out on the front of his doorstep and hasn't been discovered yet. Or better yet, maybe the police department is keeping his murder under wraps not wanting to alert the media yet until they have a suspect. The last thing the city of LA needs is another unsolved murder of a cop," I said, switching off the television.

Anxious to celebrate the demise of the once potentially toxic detective, I took a quick shower and planned a day of pampering. Yesterday, after keeping Supreme and Aaliyah out all afternoon and evening in an attempt to block the detective from speaking with him, Supreme surprised me with some cash and it was much more than what he hit me off with the first go round. He said it was to show his gratitude for taking such wonderful care of Aaliyah during these hard times and being such a good friend to him. He even made me promise that I wouldn't spend the money on anyone else but myself because I deserved it. Shiiiit, Supreme didn't have to ask me twice! I wrapped my hands around that cash with all my pearly whites showing like it was Christmas. I always knew that Supreme was generous by the way he splurged on Precious, but I had no idea that just being nice to his prized little girl would entitle me with so many perks. Aaliyah was truly an asset that I hadn't counted on.

After confirming my appointment at the beauty salon, I sashayed my ass downstairs ready to head out for my transformation. I damn near had an "Anna" moment and fell down the fucking stairs, when to my shock Detective Moore was standing in the foyer with Supreme.

That fool is supposed to be dead with a bullet to the back of his head. What the fuck happened? Devon, you have some explaining to do!

"Good morning...well I should say afternoon, Maya," Detective Moore said with a pleasant smile.

"Hi," I replied dryly. "Back so soon? I see you couldn't stay away."

"I did come back yesterday to speak to Mr. Mills. I understand you, him and the baby were out all day."

I slightly nodded my head, giving no verbal feedback.

"But today's visit is courtesy of Mr. Mills. You see he gave me a call today and I rushed right over."

"I'm sure you did. Supreme, is everything okay?" I asked, trying to disguise my annoyance with the detective.

"No, nothing is okay anymore."

"What's wrong?"

"I got a letter from Precious," he revealed with pure depression in his voice.

Yes! I cheered inside. "A letter? What did it say...is Precious alright?" I sounded so damn concerned for a second I forgot that I was the one that had the bitch on lockdown.

Supreme didn't respond, as if in a state of shock, so Detective Moore decided to be his spokesperson.

"Apparently, Mrs. Mills feels she needs some space

and isn't sure if she's coming back to her family."

"What! That doesn't sound like Precious."

"You know, Maya, I have to agree with you," Detective Moore said in an eerie way. "I met with Mrs. Mills numerous times during the kidnapping ordeal of their daughter and she didn't strike me as the type of woman who would walk away from her family. If for some reason she did want to leave she would tell you to your face not in a letter."

I felt my cheeks burning up and hoped they hadn't turned the color red. "What do you think, Supreme? Do you believe it…did Precious really write the letter?"

"It's definitely her handwriting," he acknowledged.

"But I'm going to have it submitted to our crime lab and have the validity authenticated," Detective Moore added. I expected that would happen anyway, that's why I was so fucking careful with the handling of the letter.

"I think that's a good idea. Maybe Precious didn't write it, Supreme."

"Or maybe somebody forced her to," Detective Moore said out the blue, damn near knocking the wind out of me.

"Forced her! What do you mean by that?"

"Maya, you seem like an intelligent young lady. I think you know what the word 'force' means."

"Of course I know what it means. I'm simply asking who would force Precious to write that letter and why would you think somebody did."

"Because I'm a detective and that's what we do, think of every scenario when investigating a case… especially one that is as complex as this."

If I'd been packing, more than likely I would've pulled out my heat right then and started blasting on that loose lip fool.

"Mr. Mills, I'm personally delivering this letter to the crime lab today and I'll get back to you when I find out anything."

"Thank you, I'll be waiting to hear from you."

Supreme walked Detective Moore to the door and I waited in the living room. The detective had me so worked up I had to sit down and relax. I was supposed to be acting as Supreme's rock and couldn't let him see the chips falling off my exterior. I stood up when Supreme came in the living room ready to lend my support.

"Supreme, I'm sure after the crime lab runs tests it'll reveal that Precious didn't write the letter," I said, knowing it would reveal the opposite.

"It damn sure looked like her handwriting to me. I tore this house up looking for every piece of paper Precious wrote—anything on to compare to the letter, and I know in my heart it was her handwriting."

"But what about the detective's theory that somebody forced Precious to write it?" I had to know if Supreme believed that because if he did, he would never let go and I wouldn't have a chance in the world to win his love."

"I want to believe she was forced because the thought of her turning her back on me and Aaliyah...I don't know if I could deal with that. Precious is the love of my life. What could I have done to make her stop loving me and to leave our daughter? And the only person I keep going back to is Nico."

"You think Precious could've left you for Nico?"

"I don't know, but he was the last person she spoke to on the phone and they do share some sort of sick connection."

"I know what you mean," I said as if reluctant.

"Why do you say that? Did Precious say something to you?"

"One day when we were having girl talk and discussing the men in our lives. I was saying how Clip had been my first love and I couldn't believe I fell so hard for such an evil man. She then said her first love had his own streak of evil in him. Of course that threw me off because there isn't anything remotely evil about you, Supreme."

"So what did Precious say?"

"Her comment threw me off, so I said, 'Precious, what are you talking about? Supreme is the sweetest man I've ever met. Why would you say he had a streak of evil in him?' That's when she told me she wasn't speaking about you, but of Nico."

Supreme put his head down as if he wanted to cry like a baby.

"I'm sorry, Supreme. I didn't want to hurt you. You asked me a question and you seem so torn. I only wanted to help."

"I know, Maya but I wasn't expecting to hear that. But honestly, I'm not totally surprised. If you'll excuse me, I need some time alone."

"I understand. Where's Aaliyah?"

"She's upstairs taking a nap."

"I was going to run some errands but I can stay here so when Aaliyah wakes up I can take care of her."

"That's sweet of you, Maya, but my parents are flying in today. They should be getting on my private jet any minute now."

"Oh how nice. How long are they going to be visiting?"

"Just for the day. They're taking Aaliyah back to Jersey with them. I'm going to have her stay at their house for a couple of weeks so I can handle things on my end."

"Just know that I have your back and I'll be more than willing to help you take care of Aaliyah for however long you need."

"Thank you. I might have to take you up on that when Aaliyah returns in a couple of weeks. But they miss their granddaughter and right now I have to get down to the bottom of this bullshit with Precious. With Aaliyah here I wouldn't be able to focus on this the way that I need to."

"I understand. Does that mean you want me to leave too?"

"Maya, no," Supreme said, reaching out taking my hand. "I don't know what I would've done without you. You've been a source of sanity for me these last few weeks. You can stay as long as you like. I actually welcome the company. I mean look around. This place is pretty fuckin' huge."

"Thank you, Supreme. I thought with Precious gone you might be ready for me to leave since we are best friends—or at least I thought we were. Part of me wants to believe that something bad has happened to Precious so I can understand her leaving and not telling me where she went. I too would feel betrayed if she ran off with Nico without at least telling me bye and explaining why she did it."

"I've been so caught up in how this bullshit got me fucked up that I haven't even considered your feelings. I apologize, Maya. I know Precious is like a sister to you so I know you're hurting too. You've been so strong through all this shit that I took it for granted."

"Don't apologize. We have to continue to be strong for one another and hopefully Precious will be coming back home soon." Supreme hadn't yet let go of my hand so I took it one step further and gave him a slight hug, and to my delight he reciprocated with a firm squeeze.

Damn this nigga feel good...and smell good too! I know Precious going through withdrawals missing the dick downs this fine chocolate motherfucker was stroking her with.

"Since you don't need me, I'ma head out and run my errands."

"Okay, I'll see you later on."

"Yeah, and make sure you give Aaliyah a goodbye kiss for me. Tell her Auntie Maya is going to miss her."

"I will. I know under the circumstances it will be difficult, but try and enjoy yourself today, you deserve it."

"You keep telling me that, Supreme as if you don't deserve to enjoy yourself too."

"One thing at a time," Supreme smiled before

heading to his office.

When I got in my car the first thing I did was dial Devon's number. I started the ignition, anxious for dude to pick up.

"Yo!" he said, like he had been waiting for my call. "Meet me at our spot...*now!*" I said and hung up. I kept the call short and to the point, because although I doubted it, you never knew who was listening in.

I slipped in my Year of the Gentleman CD needing to listen to some smooth R&B with all the drama unfolding, which seemed crazy since I was the one behind most of it. As I drove towards the restaurant on Robertson Boulevard, all the reasons that had brought me to this place in my life right now streamlined through my head. It all started and ended with Precious. I had these love/ hate feelings towards her. She was everything I wanted to be and had everything I wanted which made me hate her, but those very same things made me love her too. The reasoning behind this shit was so twisted that it was difficult for me to grasp sometimes. But one thing was for certain; I intended on keeping my eyes on the prize... Supreme.

When I pulled up in the parking lot I noticed Devon's car was already there. "Shit, he must've been already circling the area when I called," I said, rushing to get out of the car because I was determined to make my hair appointment.

"I can explain," Devon stood up and said as soon as he saw me coming up to the table.

I sat down, motioning him to do the same. I didn't want to draw any attention to us and his big black ass standing up as if he got busted fucking around, and trying to apologize wasn't helping.

"What, was you around the corner when I called?"

"Not exactly around the corner but close to it. I had a feeling I'd be hearing from you. But listen," Devon lowered his voice before continuing. "The reason I couldn't hit old boy off was because he came home with some honey. I guess even cops have late night booty calls. I didn't want to take no chances and have to kill both of them. Tonight though, I'm on it. He's going down, and if he got somebody with him, they going down too."

"Delete that."

"What? You don't want me to kill whoever with him too? I mean we can't leave no witnesses."

"No, I mean delete killing Moore...at least for the moment."

"Why?"

"Supreme got that letter from Precious I had her write. He took it upon himself to call in the detective. Let's just say the detective is suspicious about this so-called letter and is having it checked out at the crime lab. Of course Precious did write it and I want the detective to get the information and bring it back to Supreme. If we kill him before that it would do us more harm than good."

"But you know he's a problem. How long do you really want to keep him around?"

"Until I set a few more things in motion. You never know. The detective might become useful."

"If you say so, but I don't see how."

"You sure are singing a whole other tune. At first you didn't want any parts of taking the cat out, now you mad that I want you to cease fire."

"You made a strong argument as to why he had to go and I felt you on that. But if you want to keep him around a little longer, I'm game."

"Wonderful. But of course I'll let you know when to make your move."

"I got you. But I guess that means I won't be getting my gratitude treat anytime soon?"

"You never know, so keep your finger on the trigger. Now, I have an appointment to get to. I'll be in touch." I grabbed my purse and I was off to my next stop.

I had fifteen minutes to get to the salon, but luckily it was on North Canon Drive, which wasn't too far from where I was. The traffic was light so I breezed to the spot, and what a spot it was. This was the type of high-end establishment that you were on time for, because unless you were one of their many celebrity clients, coming late meant your name was crossed off the appointment book. The valet was waiting with a smile on his face when I stepped out of my Jag. The much younger knockoff looking Brad Pitt attendee even offered to give my car a detailed washing while I was getting my hair did, and of course I agreed.

I strolled into the sexy bungalow-style salon feeling like a star myself. I thought the place would have a typical, overrated Hollywood that thinks they are somebody aura, but it was the opposite. The staff of bleach blondes, red heads and brunettes were too friendly and almost overly accommodating, offering me everything from champagne to a personal stylist to pick out a new wardrobe to go with my new hairstyle. The life of the rich and privileged had my name written all over it.

"Miss, you can come this way," the stylist who I assumed was doing my hair said. When I sat down I fell in love with the garden terrace that was complete with fountains and rose bushes. I had a clear view because of the floor-to-ceiling windows.

"This is the life for me," I mumbled out loud.

"I'm sorry, Miss, what did you say?"

"Oh nothing, just thinking out loud."

"So what are you having done today?"

"I want some coloring, highlights and hair extensions."

"Great! Did you have a color and style in mind?"

"Yes, I even brought a picture to make your job a little easier."

"Perfect! Let me have a look," she said as I dug in my purse. I then handed her the photo and she eyed the picture and then stared at me.

"Wow, you resemble the woman in this picture an awful lot."

"Everybody says that. But it should be expected. We used to be sisters."

"Used to be?"

"Yes, her name was Precious, but she died not too long ago."

"I'm sorry for your loss."

"Thank you. I've always admired her style, but now that she's gone I think she would appreciate me carrying it on."

"That's a nice way of looking at it. They say imitation is the greatest form of flattery. So let me work my magic. First, I'll start with a scalp treatment. It's a massage of special oils and steamer."

"Sounds divine."

"It is, so sit back and relax."

It was effortless to do precisely that. I closed my eyes and let my mind travel to where I wanted to be...my life as a queen bitch. I visualized diamonds in all colors, shapes and sizes, a walk-in closet full of designer clothes, shoes and bags that even Kimora Lee Simmons would have to respect, and pushing whips that I can't even pronounce let alone spell. Each day I was getting closer to living my dream and going from nothin' to somethin'.

Precious
Walk In My Shoes

I woke up for the first time in I didn't know how many weeks without being handcuffed to a fucking bed. This new chapter in my life had now taken another bizarre turn. After Mike had fed me that delicious breakfast he kept his word and came back for lunch and dinner. Then he took another chance at letting me bathe, and this time I pulled no shenanigans. He was so impressed with all my cooperating he filled my drawers with undergarments, a few loungewear outfits and beauty products. I was almost starting to feel a sense of normalcy, if that was possible under the circumstances.

If Mike was trying to prove that what he said he was willing to do for me was true, then he was doing a damn good job. If he really wanted me to leave the country with him and I could bring Aaliyah, then I would do it. Once I got to wherever the fuck he took us, I would scheme up a plan to break the fuck out and go back to Supreme the first chance I got. But right now the most important thing was finding a way to stay alive. Playing up to Mike seemed to be the best and damn near only way to make it happen. As the idea of being reunited with Aaliyah played in my head I heard a knock at the door.

"Precious, are you up?" I heard Mike ask. What the hell, this nigga knocking now, tryna respect my privacy? Shit really has changed.

"Yeah, I'm up. Come on in, Mike." He came in carrying a tray with food and one long stem rose in a slender glass vase.

"You're feeding me another fabulous meal. You're not poisoning me on the low are you?"

"I suppose I deserve that question," Mike laughed. "But no poison. I want you alive not dead."

"Wow, pretty soon you'll let me out this bedroom and I'll be able to walk around," I joked.

"Funny you should say that. I was going to ask you if you wanted to come in the living room and watch TV or a movie."

"Mike, now you're officially buggin' me out. You have done a complete 180 in less than forty-eight hours. I get you're tryna show me a different side, but this is what one would define as drastic. Marinate on that while I eat my breakfast."

Mike sat down on the bed and got comfortable as I poured syrup on my buttermilk pancakes. I was tripping how all of sudden I went from being on the verge of starvation to being plentiful with food.

"These are bangin' and I ain't even big on pancakes," I said, savoring each bite.

"Precious, I'm sorry."

"You don't have to apologize. Like I said, they bangin'."

"I'm not talking about the pancakes."

"Then what are you apologizing for?"

"I'm sorry for raping you."

I stopped with my fork in midair. "Are you sure you want to take the conversation there, because I don't think I do."

"I understand if you don't want to say anything and simply listen."

"Do I really have a choice?"

"If you don't want to hear what I have to say then I'll end it right here."

I couldn't front, I was somewhat curious to how this clown planned on coming at me. "Go 'head."

"I never wanted to admit this, because if I did, I would have to own up to being a rapist. I've murdered, stolen, cheated, committed numerous crimes, but never did I believe I would find rapist on that list."

"Well it is."

"I know, and I'm ashamed. For so long after it happened I kept telling myself that I didn't rape you, that you wanted to have sex with me."

I put my head down because Mike and I both knew that at a point before I believed he killed Supreme, I did want to have sex with him. On one occasion

I practically begged for the dick, but none of that changed what happened the night he did rape me.

"But you didn't. You gave every indication that the last thing you wanted was for me to touch you, but instead I took it. I'll never forgive myself for that."

"Where did this big epiphany come from?"

"In my heart I knew the truth, but my mind wouldn't allow me to recognize it. I was angry for being locked up like an animal. I wanted to blame somebody and it was easy to make you the target. If I came clean and said you did nothing wrong then the only person I could blame for my demise would be me. I wasn't man enough to do that."

"But you man enough now. Forgive me if I'm not..." Mike turned around to see what had caused me to stop mid sentence.

"Isn't this cozy! My dear brother with my worse enemy!" Maya spit. "Maybe I should just kill you both right now." There was a long pregnant pause before Maya smirked. "I'm joking," she teased, placing what appeared to be a brand new designer bag on the dresser.

"What the fuck did you do to yourself?" Mike walked over to Maya with his mouth opened in confusion.

"Mike, I told you she was crazy. Maya sweetie, I hate to fracture your frame but you'll never be me. I don't care what color the hair or how long the extensions. There is only one Precious Cummings AKA Mills."

"Let's let Supreme be the judge of that."

"Maya, what are you doing? The hair, these clothes you're wearing, this ain't you."

"It's the me I've always wanted to be."

"Trick, please! Admit you want to be me. Your brother and I were just having a conversation about admitting shit, maybe you need to be a part of this."

"Damn, Mike, Precious must toss one hell of a salad because I'm assuming that's how she got you to lose your fuckin' mind. First, you move her upstairs from the basement, and now this bitch handcuff free, eating pancakes like she staying at a five star hotel instead of being a prisoner."

"I see you tryna ignore what I said, but that's cool," I commented, taking the last bite of my pancakes.

"Maya, I'm concerned about you. I know you want to win Supreme over, but turning into his missing wife might not be the move."

"Mike, fuck being concerned about me! I think you need to be concerned about yourself. Precious is playing you like she's done every other man in her life. Do you know that when she thought Supreme was dead she slept with Nico? Can't you see what type of skank she is? Her supposedly dead husband wasn't even cold in the ground and this ho was spreading her legs for the man who tried to take her out this world. And you call me the crazy one," Maya said, pointing her finger directly at me.

"Maya, that's on her. You may not agree with the choices Precious made, and I'm sure she doesn't agree with yours."

"I can't believe you're defending this tramp. She's

responsible for putting you in jail, Mike."

"No, I'm responsible for that all on my own."

I watched as the color drained from Maya's face.

"What the fuck is going on? The next thing you're gonna tell me is that you want to free this bitch and let her go home to her family." Mike remained silent which aggravated Maya further. "Fuckin' say something! Don't stand there on mute!" she screamed, raising up her hands and pushing her brother in the chest.

"Calm down," Mike said, holding Maya's arms still.

"Mike, I can't believe you're letting her do this to us. We're family! First, you set me up with that gun bullshit and now you're siding with the woman who has ruined both of our lives. What happened to us being a team?"

"Maya, how did I ruin your life? I treated you like we were blood," I interjected.

"Shut up! I don't want to hear a word out of you. This is between me and my brother."

"Maya, let's go out there and talk."

"Fuck that! Don't try that blah, blah, blah shit with me. You say what the fuck is going on right here, right now."

"Fine. In a few days I'll have that money I've been waiting for and you already know after that I'm leaving. But the thing is, I'm bringing Precious with me."

"I never thought I would think this about you, but you're a fuckin' fool. But with you holding that bullshit gun situation over my head, there isn't too much I can do about the decisions you make. Remember, when Precious leaves your dumb ass high and dry on whatever island you chillin' on to come back for her husband and daughter, don't be mad at me when I put a bullet straight through her eyes."

"She won't be coming back."

"And you're so sure because what, she's confessed her undying love for you?" Maya said sarcastically.

"Not her undying love for me, but for Aaliyah. We're bringing her with us."

"Mike, didn't you hear what I said? Precious slept with Nico too. That means he also could be the father. More than likely Aaliyah isn't even your child."

"All that is true, but what we do know is that she's Precious' child and they deserve to be together."

"I have to give it to you, Precious, you must have some unbelievable pussy. It's been how long now since my brother raped you, and he is jumping through hoops to get back between your legs, or has it already happened?"

"That's enough, Maya!"

"No, Mike, this is enough. Not only do you want to take Precious with you, but you're trying to take Aaliyah too. It doesn't matter anyway, Aaliyah's not even here."

"Where is she? Maya, so help me if you did anything to hurt my daughter…"

"Save it, Precious. Aaliyah went back to New Jersey with Supreme's parents for a couple of weeks."

"Then we'll wait for her to come back before we leave," I said, making it clear to Mike that I wasn't bouncing without my daughter.

"We can wait, that's not a problem."

"Mike, I never knew you could be so accommodating. But it doesn't matter, Aaliyah still can't leave with you."

"What's the excuse now, Maya?" Mike asked, becoming impatient.

"Aaliyah is my lifeline to Supreme. I need her here in order to win him over."

"You're never going to win him over anyway."

"Shut up, Precious. That's the last warning you'll get. You may have my brother's nose wide open but I have no problem taking you out."

"Maya, leave Precious out of this. I want Aaliyah to leave with us and that's not negotiable. You're going to have to find another way to win Supreme over."

"Here we go...once again you're deserting me like you did when I was a little girl, never protecting me, always choosing everyone and everything else over me. Neither you nor our trifling mother ever wanted to be bothered with me. For mother, she picked her pathetic boyfriends who were always itching to get a taste of my virgin pussy, and you picked your work. Always in those streets hustling not giving a damn what my life was like in that hell hole. Now I'm nineteen years old and you still don't give a damn about me. All you care about is what's best for you."

Mike and I both stayed quiet. It seemed crazy that yesterday the two of us was discussing this very topic, and here Maya was shoving it back down our throats, trying to gain sympathy votes from her brother.

"My dear brother can't be speechless. You always have some shit to pop."

"Growing up I did let you down and I carry a lot of guilt around over that. I also know that you believe I'm letting you down now, but I'm not. A mother and her daughter deserve to be together. This has to be a give and take situation. I'm giving you the opportunity to have a life with Supreme, so I have to take the one thing that means the most to Precious. The same way I have to right a wrong with you, I'm trying to right my wrong with her."

"Okay, Mike. I'll do what you've asked, but like I said, Aaliyah won't be back for a couple of weeks. That will at least give us some time to figure out how I'll give Aaliyah to you without it leading back to me."

"True. I'll brainstorm on it. Maya, thank you for doing the right thing."

"You're not giving me a choice, Mike. This is your show, so I'll play my part. You two enjoy your evening," Maya said before leaving.

Mike laid his back flat across the bed and put his hands over his face. "What the fuck happened to us?"

"Are you asking me?"

"No, I'm asking myself."

"Yeah, 'cause yah some fucked up motherfuckers. I thought I was damaged, but the Owens family got me beat."

"You don't have to rub it in, Precious."

"I mean am I really telling you something that you don't already know? The scary part is, as fucked up as your thinking is, I believe you're trying to make the best out of the horrible situation you created. Maya, on the other hand still ain't comprehending that this is some bullshit. She doesn't think she's doing anything wrong."

"I'm hoping that she'll get there."

"Nah, she ain't got no conscious. Even when I was out in them streets causing havoc I felt remorse for a few motherfuckers I had to take out. But at that moment I felt I didn't have a choice. It was like my life or theirs, so of course I chose mine. Maya don't even seem to have the capability to have remorse and that's frightening. And Mike, not too many things frighten me. Thank God Aaliyah is going to be with Supreme's parents. That will help me sleep a little bit better at night."

"I was glad to hear that too. Maya's obsession with winning Supreme over has her being erratic."

"Damn sure do, so you better be careful. Maya is determined not to let anything or anyone stop this fantasy life she's created in her mind with Supreme."

"True, but that's why I had to utilize my gun leverage."

"Would that have something to do with the cat named Terrell?"

Mike lifted his upper body off the bed and turned towards me.

"How did you know about Terrell?"

"I heard you and Maya arguing about him the other day. Who is he?" I could tell Mike didn't want to tell me which made me want to know even more. "Mike, you might as well tell me. I'm a prisoner for goodness sakes! Who am I gonna tell?"

He let out a deep sigh like fuck it. "Terrell was Nina's younger brother."

"Nina...the Nina that was engaged to Jamal and working for you?"

"Yep, that Nina."

"What is Maya's connection to him?"

"That was supposed to be her quote *man* unquote. Maya's young hot ass was in way over her head with that dude."

"What happened?"

"He was a lil' young hustling nigga from Queens makin' paper. He wasn't a major nigga in the drug game, but he fo' sho' was on a come-up makin' moves. Somehow him and Maya started dating. Again, me being so caught up in my own shit I had no idea she was dealing wit' cat, not until I got a phone call one night."

"From who?"

"Maya. She was crying being all hysterical. She told me to come get her from this townhouse in Jersey. When I got there she let me in and I see Terrell on the floor laying in a puddle of his own blood."

"What, did somebody run up in the crib and kill him?"

"Yeah, Maya's crazy ass."

"Wait a minute, Maya killed him?"

"I didn't stutter. She killed that nigga over some young girl bullshit. He was supposed to be her man and he was fuckin' around on her. The kid was only eighteen. What the fuck do you think an eighteen year old nigga, makin' money in the streets is gonna to be doing? But she was fifteen and out of her league."

"So she killed him?"

"She claimed it was an accident. That she was only tryna threaten him with the gun but it went off. I knew she was lying. I was looking in the eyes of a killer. I knew those eyes. I had them too."

"Wow, and I thought when she killed Nina it was her first time. No wonder it seemed so effortless."

"Maya killed Nina too?"

"You didn't know that? I thought for sure Maya would've told you."

"No. I always assumed you killed Nina."

"It was your sister. That was the incident that brought us so close together, because Nina was about to kill me and Maya shot her first. I had no idea that Maya even knew Nina before I introduced them."

"They didn't."

"But Maya was dating her brother."

"She was fuckin' her brother and she was just one of many. But when I saw him lying on the floor I recognized his face immediately. He used to get drugs from me and I knew he had an older sister that he was holding it down for."

"You're talking about Nina."

"Yeah, that's when I decided to recruit her. She could work for me and I would put money in her pocket now that her brother was dead because of my silly ass sister. So at the funeral I approached her and took it from there."

"Why did you hold onto the gun?"

"I know it's crazy, but I swear every time I was about to ditch that shit something kept holding me back and I'm glad I did. Trust me, if I didn't have that gun situation lingering over Maya's head there's no telling what she might do."

"So why do you fuck wit' her?"

"Unless you have your own brother or sister it's hard to explain the bond. You can be at each other's throats but you rise and fall together."

"I understand, but if you don't mind me asking, what did you do with the gun?"

Mike gave a slight laugh. "I feel like I shouldn't tell you."

"Why? It's not like I'll ever have a chance to get it. After we leave LA we're off to another country. It doesn't really matter if you tell me. I'm just curious."

"You're right, what's the harm? After Donnell did that drive by shooting for me I had him take it back to New York."

"You had that nigga take that shit all the way back to New York? How?"

"All those details aren't necessary. The point is he got it there and back to its proper resting place."

"Its proper resting place...I'm lost. Where would that be?"

"The apartment Nina lived in and Terrell paid the rent on until he was murdered. Call it twisted, but it was like my gift to Nina. When her brother died she was crushed. Me stashing it at the spot Terrell would hold down for her was like me putting the shit to rest."

"If you say so."

"But now it's even more ironic. I mean they both died at the hands of Maya. And the gun she used that could put her away for the rest of her life is stashed at a spot that both of them called home at one time."

"Who lives there now? Nina's been dead for a minute."

"I have somebody that checks up on it every now and then, but nobody. Nina always maintained that spot even after she moved in with Jamal, but it was mostly for me. The apartment was in a low key neighborhood in Queens so I would use it for some business purposes occasionally."

"So what, you keep paying the rent every month to maintain it?"

"Right before she died, Nina resigned the lease. I paid that shit up for the whole year in advance. To this day that landlord ain't neva asked no questions and don't even know that Nina is dead. When it's time to renew the lease, he puts it under the door and I get my people to pay that shit up front for the year. And you know how motherfuckers are. All they want is the loot and no tenants complaining about the noise. I'm two for two on that."

"Interesting. You better hope Maya doesn't ever find that spot."

"Nope, like I said it's a real low-key spot. She doesn't know anything about it. That's exactly the way it needs to be. Having some collateral is good because you can never be too careful. But like I said, Maya and I share a bond. It won't ever come down to that."

I heard what Mike was saying, but that so called bond he shared with Maya appeared to be one-sided to me. I wanted to be wrong because with his help I would get my daughter back. But see, I was always taught that when a man was sleeping, a woman was thinking, and in this particular case I think that applied to brother and sister too. Maya wasn't going to let anybody—including Mike—get in the way of her being able to walk in my shoes.

Maya
Prelude to a Kiss

"Ah-h-h-h-h-h-h-h!" was all I screamed for twenty minutes straight when I left from seeing my brother and Precious at the stash house. Those two motherfuckers were trying to ruin everything that I had worked so hard for. I couldn't fathom how Precious was able to turn my brother against me. *The power of pussy*, kept flashing through my brain. It had to be that because what other reason would Mike develop a conscious? I thought back to when I first started seeing glimpses of it. It all came around to Aaliyah. He had a soft spot for that little girl and for her mother. I preferred for Precious to be dead, but I was willing to let Mike ride into the night with that manipulative tramp, but not with Aaliyah too. Supreme would be devastated and would spend the rest of his life searching for her and leaving no time for me and him to become a family. I had to figure out a way to work this shit out, and it started tonight.

When I got back to the house Supreme wasn't home and Aaliyah was gone. His parents must have been in and out. I wondered what Supreme was working on that had his full attention. I knew Precious was at the center of it but I wanted the specifics. I couldn't focus on any of that right now. I didn't know how much time I was working with before Supreme would be home and I had to try and work my magic. I ran upstairs and headed straight for the shower.

It was now or never so I had to go hard. I stepped out the shower and began the completion of my transformation. It would be the tiny details that would make all the difference and I wasn't missing one. Every ten minutes I would check out the security camera to see if Supreme was pulling up, and on the fourth look I peeped his Lamborghini zooming up the driveway. My hands were shaking because I was so nervous, but there was no backing out.

I hurried down the stairs, dimming the lights and positioned myself right in front of the steel case windows. With the moonlight beaming through, the views from downtown LA to Pacific Palisades were even more spectacular.

When Supreme opened the front door, my back was facing him. I heard the door shut and his footsteps on the marble floor. His pace was quick when he first entered but became slower with each step. I knew by that, he had noticed my presence. I remained motionless as if a well sculpted wax figure. The steps got closer and closer and I was ready to jump out my skin from nervousness, but I wanted this shit to work out so damn bad I wasn't about to fuck it up.

Then I felt the strong arms I had been dying to feel, wrap around my waist. Supreme took in his favorite Dolce & Gabbana light blue scent I had purposely taken from Precious' room and sprayed on my body. He buried his face on my slender neck immersing in the seductive aroma.

"Baby, I knew you wouldn't be able to stay away. I've missed you so much. I'm so happy you're back home," Supreme whispered, gliding his hands up the silk negligee to my breasts and massaging his fingers against my hardened nipples. "Don't ever leave me again." He pressed his lips against my skin, sprinkling kisses up and down my neck. With forcefulness he turned my body around now pressing his lips on mine with eyes closed. I let our tongues intertwine and then closed my eyes too, letting my body melt in his arms. I never knew that a kiss could feel almost as good as the actual act of sex. Then it happened... all motion stopped.

"Maya, what the fuck are you doing? I thought you were Precious!" Supreme said, pushing me away. Although his voice was raised, I didn't see anger in his eyes.

"I'm sorry, Supreme. When you walked up and put your arms around me, I got caught up in the moment. Please forgive me."

"But look at you, your hair...you have on Precious'

nightgown and that perfume. That's the only kind Precious wears because she knows it's my favorite." Supreme backed away from me and sat down on the couch. "I can't believe I did what I just did."

"Supreme, it isn't your fault. I can understand how you mistook me for Precious, that's the only reason why you were attracted to me. I should've stopped you, but I didn't. I'm so wrong for that."

Supreme sat with his head down, still baffled by what happened. "Why do you look like that—like Precious?" he asked. I knew he was trying to make sense of a situation I carefully calculated.

"Well you told me to go treat myself and I decided to get a makeover. The stylist suggested the hair color and extensions. It didn't really register with me that it was so similar to how Precious wears her hair until I got home and saw all the pictures around the house. As for the negligee and perfume, Precious actually gave it to me a long time ago when I was with Clip and we were having problems. She told me this was a guaranteed way to seduce him and make him forget any other woman he may have been creeping with."

"I hear you, but this is too much."

"I know. I can't say I'm sorry enough. I haven't felt pretty in so long, and after getting pampered today I came home and wanted to feel sexy. You weren't home and I never expected for you to see me dressed in this. I only came downstairs to have a drink before going to bed, but it was like this view," I said pointing towards the window, "Was calling my name. I was daydreaming, off in another world. I didn't even hear you come in. Then when you put your arms around me and kissed my neck…" my voice trailed off. "I had no idea I was so lonely until you held me."

"You don't have to apologize, mistakes happen."

"Supreme, if for now on you're going to be feeling uncomfortable around me, I'll leave."

"What do you mean leave?"

"I'll pack up my stuff and move out. School will be starting back soon and I can get housing there in one of the dorms. Until then, I can go back to New York and visit with my mom."

"That might be for the best."

"I think so too, but is it okay if I leave tomorrow?"

"Of course. If you need for me to get you a plane ticket or anything let me know."

"I'm fine, but thanks for offering. I should head up to bed. Goodnight."

"Goodnight."

Supreme sat in the dark as I went upstairs to my room. I got in my bed feeling fucked up. That was a bold move I made, but with the walls closing in on me what was I supposed to do? Precious is somewhere on lockdown but was still winning. I fell asleep with depression and defeat engulfing my body.

Knock! Knock! Knock!

I thought that sound was coming from a dream I was having in my sleep but as it continued and became louder, I realized it wasn't the case. I slowly opened my eyes and looked at the clock on the nightstand to see what time it was. "Nine-fifteen in the morning," I said out loud, rising up in the bed. "Come in."

"Sorry to wake you up," Supreme said, standing in the doorway in a navy blue track suite.

"Supreme, I'm catching the red-eye tonight, so can I please sleep for a couple more hours before you toss me out?"

"That's the thing. You don't have to leave."

"Excuse me, but last night you told me you thought it was a good idea for me to go back to New York until school started."

"I mean you can leave if you want, but I don't want you to feel that I'm kicking you out."

"I know you're not kicking me out, but I need to leave. I was wrong, and you shouldn't feel uncomfortable in your own house to be around me."

"I don't feel that way at all."

"You don't have to ask me not to leave because you feel guilty. I'll be fine."

"It's not that," Supreme exhaled. "I don't want you to leave."

"Huh?" I sat up extra straight in the bed as if that would help me hear better.

"I want you to stay...if you want to stay."

"Honestly, I don't think I want to stay. I'll miss Aaliyah and I'm going to miss you too, but it's best if I leave." As bad as I wanted to jump up and down, I never forgot what Precious told me. First, you latch your hook into a man. Then once you got him you pull away, because all men want what they perceive they can't have.

"Why?"

"Because I crossed the line yesterday and it's best if I go."

"No you didn't."

"Yes, I did. I let you kiss me knowing you thought I was Precious."

"That's not exactly true."

"What isn't true?"

"When I first came in the house and saw you standing by the window, I did believe you were Precious. When I started kissing you though, I knew something was different, but fuck it, I'm a man and it felt good. I pushed you away because no matter how good it felt, it was wrong so I stopped myself."

Bingo! I knew I didn't see anger in Supreme's eyes when he pushed me away. "I know where you're coming from, Supreme. Precious is gone and you're lonely. It's natural that you reach out to somebody for comfort. That somebody happened to be me last night."

"Hold that thought, Maya. I'll be back in a little while. That must be Detective Moore at the door. He called a minute ago saying he would be here in a few."

"Okay, I'll be right here." Supreme rushed downstairs and I rushed out my bed so I could eavesdrop on their conversation. I knelt down at the top of the staircase and Supreme had just let Detective Moore inside.

"Can I get you something to drink?" Supreme offered, being surprisingly polite to the detective.

"No, I can't stay that long. But I wanted to come over and discuss this with you in person."

"Sure, what did you find out?"

"The lab did analyze the letter and indeed it was Mrs. Mills' handwriting."

All I could do was smile.

"I knew it!" Supreme yelled, punching the air with his fist. "How could she leave me and our daughter?" Supreme said out loud a few times before Detective Moore decided to interrupt.

"Mr. Mills, I know this is tough, but I'm still not convinced this is as black and white as it appears."

"What are you talking about? You said the handwriting is Precious'. What else could there be? My wife is probably off with Nico Carter somewhere, not giving a fuck about me or our family. Have you been able to get in touch with Nico yet?"

"No, I haven't. But because he was the last person your wife talked to on her cell, doesn't mean that she is with him."

"Why are you defending Precious so much? You don't even like her."

"I never said I didn't like Mrs. Mills, I actually somewhat admire that fiery personality of hers, but that's beside the point. As a detective, my gut tells me that there is a lot more going on here."

"What do you mean?"

"That's the thing. I can't figure it out. But I think that houseguest of yours may know a lot more than what she's saying."

My smile had now turned to a frown.

"You talking about Maya? What does she have to do with this?"

"I can't put my finger on that either, but again, my gut never lies."

"If Maya knew anything that could help us find Precious she would tell me. Precious is like a sister to her. She's just as worried about her whereabouts as I am."

"That might be the case."

"It is. Now that we know Precious is alive and well, I suppose you can close that missing person case."

"That's standard procedure, but I'll still be continuing my own private investigation, and let me know if you discover any new leads."

"I will. I appreciate your assistance, Detective, and I'm sure we'll be in touch," Supreme said, shaking Detective Moore's hand.

I scooted back to my bedroom as Supreme let Detective Moore out. I rushed into the bathroom and turned on the shower. I jumped in and let the water drench my body, then hopped back out and went to my bedroom door, peeping out of the slightly opened crack to see if Supreme was on his way up. I figured he would want to share with me his discussion with Detective Moore, and I had to do something to divert the suspicion the detective was casting in my direction. As I suspected, Supreme was coming up the stairs to see me, no doubt.

I ran back to the shower, hopped in one more time so my body would be freshly wet, and then stepped out, patiently waiting for Supreme's arrival. When I heard him knocking at my door, I ignored him, not saying a word, but willing him to come inside. He continued to knock and then called out my name. When I heard his hand on the doorknob, I ran back to the shower and turned off the water.

"Maya, are you in here?" Supreme asked, walking in my bedroom, and right on cue I made my entrance.

"Supreme, what are you doing in here!" I screamed as if embarrassed that he caught me coming out the shower butt ass naked. There is nothing like a wet glistening body to get a man's dick extra hard.

"Maya, forgive me. I knocked and called out your name but got no answer."

"Yeah, because I was in the shower and obviously didn't hear you. You need to get out, right now!" I continued my tirade.

"Of course. I'm sorry."

"You should be, now please leave. I need to get dressed."

"Sure. When you're done, please come downstairs because I need to talk to you about some things."

"Fine, now get out!" I was popping all that shit in my birthday suit without a towel in sight to cover up my tits and ass. When Supreme walked out with his head hanging down looking pitiful, I slammed the door and locked it as if I was done with him. How proud and pissed Precious would be. I was using every trick she ever taught me to score her own husband.

I took my time getting dressed, purposely making Supreme wait. I hoped this new drama I conjured up would scoot out that bullshit Detective Moore had left on his brain. To be on the safe side, I added an extra prop. I walked slowly down the stairs carrying my suitcase. The way Supreme's eye bulged, I knew he was thrown for a loop.

"Why do you have your suitcase? I thought we decided you were going to stay."

"No, you said I could stay and I've decided not to."

"Why?"

"What did you want to talk to me about?" I asked, intentionally switching the subject.

"Oh yeah, umm...the letter."

"What letter?"

"The one I got from Precious."

"You mean the fraudulent letter that someone must've forged?"

"No, it wasn't forged. She wrote it."

"What!" I dropped my suitcase to the floor for a dramatic affect.

"I know. In my heart I wanted to believe she didn't write it, but my head kept telling me she did."

"I can't believe it! Why would Precious leave you and Aaliyah? You seemed like the perfect family. I admired your relationship so much. I hoped that I would share that type of love with someone, someday."

"I thought we were the perfect family too. I don't know where I went wrong."

"What else did the detective say?" I inquired to see if he would mention the suspicions the detective had about me.

"Nothing really. They're going to close out the missing person case, but he's still going to do his own investigating."

"Why?"

"You know detectives. They never give up until they have all the answers."

"What are you gonna do?"

"Honestly, I don't know. My first priority is to make sure Aaliyah is happy. It's good that she's with my parents right now."

"I hope everything works out for you and Aaliyah, but I need to be going."

"I thought your flight didn't leave until tonight."

"It doesn't, but I have to take care of a few things."

"Maya, I really am sorry about what happened earlier. I hope that isn't why you're leaving."

"I was angry at first, but when I thought about it, I know you didn't mean to walk in on me naked. I'm leaving because with Precious gone and now that I know she may not come back, there's really nothing left for me here. I was thinking of even enrolling in a college in New York instead of coming back to LA."

"Is that what you want?"

"I only came to LA to be with Clip and because Precious was here, but now that they're both gone, why should I stay? For all I know, Precious could be back in New York. You know she will always be a Brooklyn girl at heart."

"You think Precious could really be in Brooklyn?"

"Hell, I don't know, but ain't Nico from Brooklyn also?"

"So you think she ran off with Nico too?"

"I'm sorry, Supreme, that was insensitive of me to even mention Nico. I was voicing my thoughts out loud. I'm trying to understand what or who would make Precious abandon her life here in LA with you."

"I was contemplating the same shit and I keep coming back to Nico. The fucked up part is that nigga seems to have fallen off the face of the earth too."

"I'm confused. What are you talking about?"

"I've had my own team of topnotch private investigators hunting that nigga down and it's like he's ghost. The last lead was him setting up shop in Chicago. Now they can't locate that motherfucker nowhere. I'm wondering if him and Precious done ran off to some island somewhere. But best believe, I don't know when, but one day both of them will have to answer for this shit, I guarantee that."

"I feel you, Supreme, and I wish you the best of luck."

"I appreciate that. I hate to see you go but you have to do what's best for you. Call me when you get to New York. Let me know you got there safely."

"I will. I'll talk to you later. Bye, Supreme."

"Bye, Maya."

Bye, my motherfuckin' ass! My sweet, innocent persona was working beautifully on Supreme. I walked out the front door to the estate more confident than ever with my position in his life. This nigga was a wounded dog. He was convinced that his ride and die bitch, Precious had tossed him to the side to ride off with the next dude. There was no one more vulnerable than a heartbroken, lonely man. Last night's prelude to a kiss was only the beginning.

Precious
Boss Man

I eyed the clock, and I knew Mike would make his appearance at any moment. We were on some sort of set schedule now. I already had breakfast and he would give me a snack an hour or so before lunch. With this new arrangement, Mike was becoming more lax with each passing day. He wasn't allowing me to walk the house freely—yet, but I had a feeling it would be happening soon.

"Come in," I said when I heard Mike knocking at the door, looking forward to the treat of the day. That was something I never thought would happen. But being dead in the center of this shit I see now how hostages become brainwashed by their captors. You seriously start appreciating whatever kind gesture they show you. Technically you know it's some bullshit, but your head be so fucked up, you'll take the shit anyway you can get it.

"Where's my snack?" I asked, feeling an instant letdown when Mike came in the room with nothing in his hand, not even a glass of water.

"I thought maybe today you would like to come in the kitchen and eat your snack."

"Seriously, or are you gonna change your mind again? Yesterday you invited me to come watch a movie then backtracked when I took you up on the offer. Is this round-two of the teasing?"

"No teasing, come with me and see for yourself."

I let my leg dangle from the bed for a few seconds giving Mike a chance to say "Sorry, the jokes on you, you ain't going anywhere", but when he didn't, I got the fuck up ready to bolt. Any chance I got to step away from the depression of being stuck in a room, I jumped at.

"So this is where you whip up all my meals," I said, looking around the hi-tech kitchen.

"This is it. Now have a seat." Mike went to the stainless steel refrigerator and pulled out a fruit platter. "Do you like Jamaican fruit punch?" he asked getting a couple of glasses out of the cabinet.

"I never had any."

"Today will be your first time then. I think you'll enjoy."

I didn't care to drink or eat anybody's shit, but hell, the worst thing that could happen was Mike would poison me and I'd die. And the odds were stacked against me in that favor anyway.

I nibbled on the sweet melon and sipped on my punch, sizing up Mike's every move. "Mike, you seem to be in an awfully good mood today. What's up?"

"Maybe knowing that soon I'll be out of LA a free man and a lot richer is making these last few months being on the run worthwhile."

"You know, I've been meaning to ask you how you pulled that off."

"Pulled what off?"

"Breaking out of Clinton Correctional Facility. That ain't no low-level prison. They pretty tight with security, so how in the fuck did you pull it off?"

Mike stopped in the middle of spreading Miracle Whip on a sandwich he was making and glanced up at me with a devilish smirk. "I don't know if I really need to be discussing that with you."

"Back to that again. Like I said before, who the fuck can I tell?" I said, discreetly scanning the room to see if I could spot a phone anyplace, but no luck. Besides the knife Mike was holding to spread his dressing, I didn't see any useable objects that could stand in as a weapon.

"True, but some things are best left not being discussed."

"Come on, Mike, stop being so secretive and share the inside scoop," I smiled, trying to soften him up.

"Real talk, it wasn't that complicated."

"Okay, so spill."

"When Maya was setting this shit in motion she brought Devon on board. She showed him a picture of me, and Devon said this dude he used to run with could damn near pass for my twin. Of course I didn't believe that shit and neither did Maya."

"I bet yah did when you got a look at that nigga. Because when I laid eyes on the dude, I was a believer."

"Fo real! Yo, when Maya showed me his pic all I could do was say 'Damn!'. Luckily he was down for the switch too for the right price."

"He was willing to do the whole bid for you? I can't imagine no price being right for that."

"Nah, he wasn't supposed to be in there that long. Just enough time for me to get the fuck out the country, but of course you fucked that shit up when you came to the prison and busted him."

"Don't even go there. Let's get back to your story. You say dude wasn't supposed to be there that long. How was yah gonna get him out?"

"Now you know I had inside help. How else do you think I was able to pull the shit off in the first place? Big time dealer I used to do business with had a brother that was a security guard at the prison. When the imposter came to see me for a visit he was dressed incognito. The guard let him go to the bathroom first and I went in after. He tossed me his street clothes in exchange for my prison attire. After that, there was no looking back."

"That shit sound simple as hell."

"Shit is simple when you got money and know motherfuckers in the right places. It's too bad that you busted dude, because when the security guard got word, he was supposed to get homeboy the fuck outta there. Now that nigga stuck doing his own bid behind the shit."

"Why you looking at me like I'm the cause of that

shit? Didn't nobody tell yah to orchestrate a prison break. I was tryna get my daughter back, that's all."

"I know, but still..."

"Still nothing. Shit, when you got the fuck out of that prison, I doubt you was bit more thinking about when and if that imposter was going to get caught or when he would be freed."

"You right. When I tasted freedom, I said they would have to kill me before I ever got caged up like an animal again."

"I bet you did." Right when I was about to throw some more questions Mike's way I heard the doorbell.

"He can't be here this early," Mike said, looking down at his watch.

"Who can't be here?"

"The money man I'm closing out my dealings with. Listen, I need you to go back to the bedroom. You can come back out when I'm done."

"I can stay in here. You don't have to worry about me blowing up your spot."

"I ain't worried about that. This is my man. We've made a lot of paper together. He wouldn't turn on me no matter what you said to him."

"So then why can't I stay right where I'm at?"

"Because I'm handling business and don't need no interruptions. So would you go back to your room, please?"

The doorbell started ringing again and Mike was rushing me off. I headed to the bedroom knowing damn well that I would be listening my ass off.

I closed the door shut extra loud so Mike would

think I was safely stashed in the bedroom. I tried to peep around the hallway corner to get a look at the man as he walked towards the living room with Mike, but all I could see was his shoes—a slick pair of smoke gray Gucci loafers.

"Quentin, my man! I appreciate you coming all the way from New York to bring me this paper."

"Not a problem. I needed a change of scenery anyway. All work and no play is never any good, especially for a player."

"And no doubt you are definitely a player." The two men both gave a slight laugh. "Can I get you a drink or anything?" Mike offered.

"Just a glass of water for me. I have some more business to handle with a new connect named Genesis when I leave here, so I want to keep a clear mind."

"Always on your job, Quentin."

"Got to. How else do you think I continue to be the boss of these streets for over twenty years?"

"I feel you, man. When I grow up I want to be just like Quentin Jacobs."

"You on your way."

"Nah, this is it for me. I'm officially out the game. I got the cash I need, and now it's time for me to get the hell outta LA—shit, make that the US."

"I hate shit got to end like this for you. Not able to show your face, on the run, that ain't no kinda life."

"It's better than being locked up in a prison wit' some punk ass guards telling me what the fuck to do twenty-four-seven. It may not be the freedom I want, but it's damn sure the freedom I need to get by day after day. Now with all this loot, I'm good."

"What is Maya going to do now? Who is going to look after her?"

"Maya is a survivor, she'll be fine."

"She's a young girl. I know she needs help."

"You always concerned about Maya and you ain't neva met her but what, twice? Let me find out you gotta thing for my sister. You know I have much respect for you, Quentin, but you a little too old to be sniffing after Maya." Both men laughed in unison again.

"It's nothing like that. I remember you mentioning that she wasn't close to her mother and you were the only family she had. Now that you'll be gone, I know things might be somewhat difficult for her. I was offering my help if she needs it."

"That's good lookin' out, and it means a lot to me."

This Quentin character had me curious. I wanted to get a close-up on this man who seemed to be a crooked nigga with a heart of gold. I mean why else would he give a fuck about Maya's reckless ass. I knew Mike would be pissed the fuck off, but I had to match a face with the deep baritone smooth voice. I tip-toed closer to the male voices coming from the living room and not making my presence felt until I walked right up on them.

"Mike, sorry to bother you but I need to use the restroom." Mike and Quentin both stared in my direction.

"Then go. You know where the bathroom is," Mike said, with annoyance in his voice.

"I just wanted you to know that's where I would be in case you came looking for me."

"Thanks," Mike replied, turning his face back towards Quentin.

"Do I know you?" Quentin asked, brushing past Mike and coming towards me. He reached out his arm and we shook hands. He was ridiculously handsome, especially for a man with some age on him. He appeared to be a well preserved, in the upper 40ish age range. If you went by his wheat brown chiseled face and tall lean body, he could've easily passed for mid-thirties, but he maintained an old school aura with a sophisticated flare that only age and living could bring you.

"No, you don't."

"You look awfully familiar. What's your name?"

"Precious Mills."

"Mills...I don't know any Mills."

"Like I said, you don't know me. Well, I need to go to the bathroom. Excuse me," I said, breaking free from the strong grasp he had on my hand.

"She reminds me of a woman I used to know a long time ago," I heard Quentin say as I walked down the hallway towards the bathroom.

When I got to the bathroom, I closed the door and turned on the sink faucet. I sat down on a chair pushed against the wall, getting my aggravation under control. I had so many emotions running around inside. I didn't know if it was Mike or Quentin that had me infuriated, or maybe both. But it had to be Quentin. I had already been through the *I Hate Mike* phase twenty

million times. What about Quentin had gotten so under
my skin? He hadn't been rude to me, in fact he was
no doubt a charismatic cat. But when he shook my
hand, the vibe was off. Maybe I was pissed that he was
concerned about Maya, but then it wasn't like he knew
that trifling heifer was doing her best to steal my life,
the life I busted my ass to get. It was something else,
but I couldn't put my finger on it.

Knock! Knock! Knock!

"Precious, you can come out the bathroom now,"
Mike said through the door.

"I'll be out in a minute."

"No, come out now, and I hope you ain't up to
nothing stupid."

"Oh please! Ain't nobody hatching shit up," I said,
turning off the water. Shit, I learned my lesson from
my first attempt at freedom. Unless I had a gun or
a big fuckin' knife, my odds of overpowering Mike
were nil. I opened the door and there was Mike
standing in front with his own gun in hand.

"We back to that again?" I questioned, looking
down at his weapon and then rolling my eyes.

"I couldn't take any chances."

"Mike, please. You can put the gun away. You
promised that you would get my daughter for me, so
I'm not gonna do nothing to fuck that up."

"Then why did you come out the room and
interrupt my business meeting?"

"It didn't sound like no meeting to me. Ya sounded
more like old friends."

"That's not the point. I told you to stay in the

bedroom until I was done."

"I had to use the bathroom. What was I supposed to do, wet my pants?"

"Whatever! Your mother must've never taught you that a hard head make for a soft ass."

"Nah, I didn't have those types of conversations with my moms. But seriously, Mike, you can put that gun away. It ain't called for."

"Cool, but stop being difficult. You had been playing your position with ease, then the minute company show up you wanna show your ass."

"Speaking of company, how you know that Quentin dude? He seem a bit old to be a lil' nigga you was kicking it with on the playground."

"Funny, but he was the man that put me on."

"Put you on in the drug game?"

"Yeah."

"How did that happen?" I questioned, following Mike back into the kitchen.

"Damn, that was so many years ago, I couldn't have been no more than fourteen or fifteen years old. My moms had just had Maya and we were struggling. With no man around I had to step up to the plate and put some food on the table."

"What about Maya's father? Where was he at?"

"I told you, my moms never told me who Maya's father was. But I knew it wasn't my dad because he had been out the picture long before Maya was even conceived."

"True. So how did you meet Quentin?"

"Everybody on the streets of New York had heard of Quentin Jacobs. This was the first man we knew of that was not only moving major drugs, but pimping women too. We all worshipped that nigga. So one day when I was standing on the corner in front of the bodega with my dudes, Quentin pulled up in a spankin' new Benz. He rolled down his window and signaled for me to come over. For a minute I didn't move because I couldn't believe he was asking for me. Then he called out my name and I leaped to the car. You didn't keep a nigga like Quentin Jacobs waiting."

"How did he know your name?"

"I wanted to know the same shit but felt it best not to question him. Me and my nigga was always in some bullshit around the way and I figured he heard about us being on some menace to society type shit."

"I can see that."

"But, umm, like he had heard my prayers. When I got to his car, Quentin offered me a chance to work for him. He started me off on some low level gofer type shit, but I followed his directions meticulously without ever fucking up, and soon my pockets stayed thick. After that my mother and Maya never had to worry about food, clothes or shelter again. I became the man of the house and shit was straight all thanks to Quentin Jacobs."

"That's some story. Quentin was the family savior."

"No doubt, and he still the savior now. Even when I got locked up he was helping me make moves from behind bars. He made arrangements for me to be able to stay in this house. Now he came through with this money I need and I'm straight."

"Shit, everybody needs a friend like Quentin."

"We more than friends. Quentin said I was always like a son to him and he definitely became like the father that was never there for me."

"He don't have no kids of his own?"

"He is married and he does have kids with his wife, but he don't really talk about them. He keeps them shielded, out the life. As long as I've known Quentin, I've never been to his house or met his family."

"Wow, talk about keeping shit on the low."

"Yeah, that's probably why he's been able to stay on top of the game for all these years. Can't nobody fuck wit' you if they don't know how to get to you. But enough talk about Quentin. Let's eat."

I watched as Mike put some plates and silverware on the table, and although I was hungry my mind remained fixated on Quentin. Something about him was intriguing and it just wasn't because he was a boss man.

Maya
Up In Smoke

"What are you doing here? I thought you were on a plane to New York."

"I missed the flight," I lied as I stood in Supreme's bedroom doorway.

"What time is it?" Supreme eyed the clock and I noticed the half empty bottle of liquor on his nightstand.

"I hope you don't mind that I came back here, but I had nowhere else to go," I said, moving slowly towards his bed.

"Why are your clothes wet?"

"It's pouring down rain outside."

Supreme stared up at the skylights and saw the rain splashing against the glass. "You're right, I'ma little out of it."

"That's okay, you've had a rough day."

"You mean a few rough days."

"Yeah, but it'll get better," I said, stroking my fingers on the back of his head.

"You should go change and get out of those wet clothes before you get sick."

"Supreme, you're always so concerned about everybody else. I don't know how Precious could've ever left you. But you're right, I do need to get out of these clothes. I peeled out of my ultra teal, off-the-shoulder jersey dress, and let it drop to the floor. I stood in front of Supreme with only my cream lace thong and three-inch jeweled thong sandals.

"Maya, what are you doing?"

"I think it's pretty obvious," I said slipping, off my panties. "It's okay to want me because I want you too." I lifted the blanket from Supreme and his fine ass was already naked. That nigga had sculpted muscles from his shoulders down, but the most important muscle was sticking straight up hard as hell, ready to fill up my wet pussy.

"Maya, we can't do this! It ain't right!"

"You let me worry about what is right," I said, wrapping my other lips around his solid long, thick tool. I stroked my tongue up, down and around his dick before focusing my tongue action on the tip of the head.

"Damn, Maya!" Supreme moaned, leaning his head back.

"I know you want this pussy," I purred, knowing he hadn't fucked since Precious disappeared. I knew he was horny as hell and I was taking full advantage. Like a vampire needing a blood fix, Supreme reached for me and devoured my neck with passionate kisses until finding his way to my breasts. He was sucking on them so hard it almost felt like bites, but the roughness of the shit was turning me on. Supreme cupped my ass with his hands and jammed his humongous dick inside of me. I screamed so fucking loud I thought the glass would shatter.

"Maya, do you want me to stop?"

"No, please don't stop! This dick feels so good! I can take it!" And I could. Shit, if I had my way I would be taking this dick on a regular. Now all I had to do was get rid of Precious once and for all.

****

"I got your message. What's so urgent?" Devon asked as he sat across from me in our regular meeting spot.

"There's been a change of plans and I need your help to execute it."

"Does that mean we're back to taking out the detective?"

"Not yet. That might not be necessary."

"You sure?"

"I ain't never sure about shit until after it happens, but we need to handle Precious first."

"Precious? Mike told me he had that situation under control."

"When did you talk to Mike?"

"The other day I went by to see him."

"And what did he tell you?"

"That Precious and the baby were leaving the country

with him. They were waiting for Aaliyah to come back and they were out. He said he already discussed it with you."

"Yeah, he did but I never agreed to it, and I'm not agreeing to it now. Precious has to go."

"Hell, I don't give a fuck either way. I don't even like that chick, so I'm down for however you want to move forward."

"Good, that's what I wanted to hear. Let's head over to the stash house and we can discuss it further in the car."

****

After discussing the plan with Devon on our drive over to the house, I then thought about how relieved I would be to get rid of Precious and no longer feel I was living in her shadow. That wasn't possible as long as she was alive. Her death was my only solution. Even after Supreme and I had that incredible night of sex I knew Precious was heavy on his mind. Even though he believed his wife left him for the next nigga, he was still mourning her ass. The shit was about to drive me crazy. I was going to take great pleasure putting us both out of our misery.

"Maya," Devon huffed.

"*What!*" I said with an attitude because I didn't like how he called my name.

"I've been trying to get your attention for the last few minutes. We're here."

"Oh," I said, seeing the house out of the backseat window. "You remember the plan, right?"

"Of course. Shit, I'm ready."

"Well get what you need from the trunk."

"Already did that while you was spacing out."

"Funny! Let's go then."

When we walked in the house Mike and Precious were lounging in the living room watching television like they was a fucking married couple.

"Isn't this cute, love in the afternoon," I mocked at my simple ass brother.

"What yah doing here? We ain't got no meetings on the calendar," Mike said, getting up from the couch.

"Oh, now that you're playing house with Precious, I need a reason to come visit my big brother?"

"Maya, don't start with the bullshit today. I'm not in the mood."

"I hope you're in the mood for something else."

"Something else like what?"

"Excuse me, Mike, do you mind if I get something to drink from the kitchen?" Devon asked, reciting his line perfectly.

"Go head, man, help yourself."

"Thanks. Maya, do you want something?"

"No, I'm good. I have some things to discuss with my dear brother, that's all." I watched as Precious was eyeing the situation and Devon's movements. That bitch wasn't stupid. She knew some shit was up.

"Spill it, Maya. What's so fuckin' important that you had to stop by on a sunny Saturday afternoon?"

"That's no sort of greeting for your sweet younger sister."

"Maya, we both know there is nothing sweet about you."

"I think Supreme would disagree with that." I saw Precious balling her fist as she sat on the couch, no doubt ready for an all out beat down, but she would have to hold tight—I would get to her in a minute.

"If you came over here to fuck with Precious about Supreme, you can leave with that bullshit. We already discussed this shit, and she knows Supreme is all yours. We don't need you coming over here rubbing that shit in her face."

"Aren't you the superhero. But sorry, your kryptonite has run out."

"What the fuck are you babbling about? I don't like word play."

"We're sticking to the original plan. Precious has to go… today."

"I told you she was gonna try this shit, Mike. Maya won't feel content until she knows I'm dead."

"Precious, nobody ever said you weren't a smart girl. You know we both can't be walking this earth, one of us has to go, and unfortunately that's you."

"You lowdown, pathetic piece of shit!" Precious spat, now standing next to Mike.

"Both of ya calm down. Ain't nobody doing nothing. Maya, Precious is leaving with me and you're leaving this house. The only time I want you to come back is when you're bringing Aaliyah so we can get the fuck outta here."

"You're not getting it, Mike. I'm not bringing Aaliyah, and Precious is going to die, today."

"I ain't letting that happen, Maya,"

"I had a feeling you were going to say that."

"Mike, watch out!" Precious screamed, but her warning was too late. Devon had already used his stun gun to knock Mike out. Precious then kicked Devon in the crotch area in an attempt to get the stun gun out of his hand.

"Back the fuck up!" I said, pulling out the .44 magnum I was packing. "Devon, you handle my brother and I'll tend to Precious. Get to walking, G.I. Jane, before I bust a cap in your ass," I directed.

"Maya, somehow, someway you gon' pay for this shit."

"One things for sure, the payback won't be from you because soon you'll be on your way to hell. Now get the fuck in that room." I shoved Precious in the bedroom and locked the door.

"You *will* get yours!" Precious yelled out through the door. She could scream all she wanted because all that was coming to an end.

"First thing first," I said, going back to the scene of the crime. Devon had already carried Mike downstairs to the basement. Mike was a solid nigga, but Devon was a humongous gorilla dude, so lifting him was lightweight work.

"Hand me the cuffs," Devon said, as he chained up Mike's feet. "He already starting to come too." I tossed Devon the handcuffs, not wanting no fuckups.

"Yo, what the fuck happened?" Mike said, shaking off his few minutes of a blackout.

"Dear brother, I'm so sorry it had to come to this."

"Maya, why the fuck do you have me chained up?" he asked, realizing the tables had turned and he was now the prisoner. "No, you can't be doing this. And

Devon, you in on this bullshit too?"

"Of course he is. He works for me, I hired him, remember?"

"So what, you wanna lock me up so I can stay out the way while you kill Precious? And then what?"

"Actually, you got it backwards. We're going to kill you first and then Precious."

Mike's entire face dropped, and for a brief second my heart ached for him. "Maya, I'm your brother. We're blood."

"I know, and it does pain me that I have to kill you too, but you've made all these demands that I can't accommodate."

"What demands?"

"For one, letting that bitch live. I always knew in some way that Precious would be your downfall. I remember the first time I saw you two together, and I had never seen you look at a woman like that before. It was as if you were completely infatuated with her, almost obsessed. Now you see where your obsession has gotten you...a death sentence."

"No, it's your obsession that has led to this, and it's what will be the end of you. It's a damn shame how bad you want to be Precious. Having her husband isn't enough for you, you want her daughter and her life. Precious warned me that you'd turn on me too, but I didn't believe her. I refused to see how far gone you really were. Maya, don't do this. There is no turning back if you kill me."

"You stupid fuck, I don't want to turn back! I'm about to have the life I've dreamed of. Too bad you won't be around to see it. But you can give me a going away present."

"And what would that be?"

"Where's the gun, Mike?"

"Wouldn't you like to know?"

"You're going to die anyway, you might as well tell me. I'll make you a deal. If you tell me where the gun is, I won't torture Precious before I kill her."

"What happened to you? I know I'm a fucked up individual, but you're on a whole other level."

"I guess I'm the worse case scenario of what happens when a little girl grows up without her father's love, or her mother's for that matter. Or maybe no love at all, because I didn't have yours either."

"Yes, you did. I was a kid myself. I did the best I could."

"No you didn't. I was never your first priority. You chose the streets over me and now a woman like Precious. Fuck both of you!" I said, blasting off putting the lights out for my brother. When his brains splattered on the concrete wall I didn't even shed a tear.

"That was quick," Devon said, seemingly in shock at how I had no qualms about killing my own brother.

"Yeah, now come on. The next round is what I'm really looking forward to."

When we got upstairs to the bedroom where Precious was stashed, she was banging on the door as if help was going to come for her ass.

"Devon, kick that motherfucker door down," I whispered so Precious wouldn't have time to get out the way. Devon's big ass put all his might in that kick and the door flew open, knocking Precious' ass across the room. "We're back!" I hummed.

"Where's Mike?" Precious wanted to know as she tried to pick herself off the floor.

"Mike is no longer with us. He sends his love."

"You killed him, didn't you?"

"You already know the answer to that."

"Killing your own brother is low even for you, Maya."

"Devon, grab a hold of this bitch for me."

"Don't fuckin' touch me!" Precious yelled and screamed, swinging her arms and kicking up her legs trying to put up a decent fight, but she was no match for Devon's monstrous ass.

"Give it up, Precious."

"Yeah, before I break your neck," Devon warned, getting tired of the little but painful jabs she was putting in. Devon now had Precious all wrapped up with her arms behind her back and legs held between his.

"Perfect!" I said, slipping on some old school brass knuckles and commenced to beating the shit out of her. "Take that, ho!" I said with a left hook then right hook, sending blood gushing from her mouth with each swing of her jaw. I then further punished her with body shots.

"Fuck you!" Precious managed to say even while I was beating her ass. It incensed me even more that she wouldn't bow down, even under all this duress.

"So you know that's what me and Supreme was doing the other night. He fucked me so good, I'm still on a high. I'll keep sucking his dick just right, and soon he'll be like 'Precious who?'"

"You can whistle on his balls and I'll still be in

that nigga's heart. For Supreme and me it's love for life..." were the last words Precious spoke as my final blow sent her to her deathbed.

"Drop her ass!" I ordered Devon. Precious fell to the floor and blood was coming out of her mouth and nose and it even looked to be seeping out of her ears. I fucked up her face so bad she was unrecognizable. "Come on, let's burn this motherfucker down and get the fuck outta here.

As we poured gasoline around the crib, I searched for the gun I wanted from Mike but came up empty. "You ready?" I asked Devon, giving up on my search and ready to get the fuck out.

"Yeah, let's light it up and get the fuck out."

"Hold on a minute, let me check out something real quick." I noticed a black leather suitcase on the kitchen table. When I clicked open the locks my eyes lit up like a Christmas tree.

"What you see?"

"Oh nothing, just some paperwork, but I better take it just in case some important documents are inside."

"Cool, but we need to go. Our business is done here."

Before Devon and I made our exit, I stood in the entrance and lit a match, and it was up in smoke for that motherfucker.

Precious
Hello Brooklyn

"Is anybody in here?" I heard somebody screaming out. "If somebody's in here, make some noise so I can find you." The voice was clear, but it was as if mine was on mute. In my head I was yelling out for help, but my entire face was in so much pain I couldn't even move it. I literally had no strength left in me, but I had to find some. I had to fight to live so I could get back home to my family and to destroy Maya. With all my force I crawled to the door. It felt like I was moving as slow as a snail, but I was making progress.

"Help me!" I cried out, being barely audible. I could feel the burning heat from the floor, and that's when I realized the house was on fire. My face was so fucked up that my nostrils couldn't even smell shit. I picked up my pace determined to live. I gave one final push into the hallway and then I blacked out again.

****

"Where am I?" I moved my arm, and a pain shot through my body that sent me into a fetal position. I slowly lifted my shirt to see what the cause of all my pain was, and my entire torso was covered in bandages.

"Precious, you woke up," I heard a familiar voice say. But my eyes were swollen shut and my vision was blurry. The harder I focused to see the image, the more my head would start throbbing.

"Who are you? What happened to me? Where am I?" the questions kept rolling of my tongue.

"It's okay, baby. I'ma take care of you."

"Nico, is that you?" I asked, wanting to break down and cry. I felt as if I didn't know myself anymore.

"Yes, baby, it's me. You're safe now."

"What happened? Where am I?"

"You're in Brooklyn."

"How did I end up back in New York? I have to get back to LA and be with my family." Flashes of Devon holding me down as Maya beat the shit out of me had my voice sounding hysterical. That deranged bitch whipped my ass so bad she had me about to go crazy.

"Precious, you have to calm down. You are in no condition to go anywhere. We have to get you well first, and then you can go back to your family. But first I want you to tell me who did this to you. Was it Mike?"

"Oh God, Mike! Mike is dead."

"What? So if Mike didn't do this, then who?"

"His sister."

"Maya? Wasn't she the girl that killed Nina?"

"Yes, that crazy fuckin' Maya. She killed Mike too."

"Her brother?" he questioned as if he believed I was delusional.

"Yes, her brother. If I told you the nightmare I've been stuck in for the past few weeks, it would blow your mind, and Maya's sick ass was behind the whole thing." It was evident by the silence in the air that Nico still wasn't getting it.

"Precious, it's clear you've been through hell, ain't no disputing that. But you're telling me that Maya— Mike's little sister—is the cause of your predicament?"

"Yes, that's exactly what I'm fuckin' saying."

"I know how you get down, and ain't no way Maya got you looking fucked up like this."

"Of course she had help, but she's behind all this bullshit. Man, she been plotting this shit against me for I don't know how long. All I know is she got Mike out of jail, helped orchestrate the kidnapping of Aaliyah, and this crazy bitch is determined to not only see me dead, but take my fuckin' life, literally, which includes my husband. That's why I got to get the fuck outta here," I said, trying to get out of bed. "Oh shit!" I grabbed my side, bending over in pain.

"Yo, you need to rest," Nico said, laying me back down on the bed.

"How can I rest knowing that psycho is playing house with my family?"

"We can deal with Maya after we nurse you back to health."

"Nico, I haven't even thanked you for saving my life."

"Don't thank me, thank the man upstairs," Nico said, pointing his index finger towards the ceiling. When I saw that house burning down I had no idea you were in there."

"What brought you to that house?"

"When we were on the phone that day and you went silent, I kept calling you back but got no answer. My gut told me something was wrong, but I wasn't sure what. I thought maybe Supreme had walked up on you and maybe you didn't want him to know you were speaking to me. The shit was buggin' me out. Then I called you a few days later and your phone kept going straight to voice mail. But when some detective dude…"

"You mean Detective Moore?"

"Yep, that's his name. When he left me a couple of messages saying he wanted to ask me a few questions regarding your whereabouts, I knew some serious shit was up. I mean dude wasn't going to be calling me unless some shit popped off. And for him to even have been able to get my number, I knew he must've traced it back from my cell phone call to you."

"Right, so did you ever call him?"

"Hell no! You know I don't fuck wit' no police. But what I did do was make some calls to find out if anybody knew what the fuck was going on. Didn't nobody really have no answers. All they kept on saying was Mike was still on the run and last they heard he was in LA. Then finally I got a break.

There's this nigga named Quentin Jacobs that has been in the game forever. Motherfuckers call him like the Godfather."

"It's a small world. I met that cat."

"When?"

"He came to see Mike."

"Well that's the break I got. His right hand man is my people. He told me Quentin had been in touch with Mike and went to LA to close out some business and give him some loot because Mike was breaking out for good. He gave me the location and I'm hauling ass cause I'm thinking this my last chance to ever find out what the fuck happened to you, so I chartered a plane. I was prepared to go LA and kill that nigga."

"Nico, thank you for caring."

"Fuck, is you crazy? Baby girl, you gon' always be my heart."

When I thought about how fucked up I must look and for Nico to say something like that, it made me realize that shit could be a lot worse right now. "Thank you."

"I have nothing but love for you, baby, don't ever forget that."

"I won't."

"But back to how I found you. So my man gave me the location, and when I pulled up, the crib was up in smoke and I swear I thought I had the wrong address. I was about to break the fuck out."

"Why didn't you?"

"That's why I told you to thank the man upstairs,

because something kept pulling me back to that house. I couldn't bring myself to leave. Precious, when I saw you I was afraid I had lost you for good."

"I can imagine how fucked up I looked when you found me. Shit, for a minute I thought I was dead too."

"Luckily I have some dealings with these Dominican cats in LA. They told me to take you to this private doctor they all fuck with if one of their crew members get fucked up during some criminal shit and they don't want to take them to the hospital. "

"So that's who bandaged me up."

"Yeah, he pretty much saved your life."

"No, you did that, Nico."

"Okay, well he followed my lead. He also prescribed you some medicine for the pain, which you're going to take after I feed you this soup. Precious, I know you're a fighter, but you won't be able to win the war if you don't let me take care of you."

"I know. I can't go back to LA looking like this anyway. I would scare the shit out of Aaliyah and Supreme wouldn't recognize me. I need to get strong."

"I'm glad you get that."

"Shit, I don't have a choice. I can barely get out of bed...forget about walking."

"What in the fuck did Maya do to you?"

"She had her flunky, Devon hold me while she hammered my face and body with her fists. To make it even more painful, she wore brass knuckles on both hands."

"Damn, that's brutal," Nico said, shaking his head.

"Maya will get hers though."

"I'm sure. If I was a betting man, I would no doubt put my money on you."

"Good choice. Right now all I want to do is get better and look halfway normal again."

"You will. The doctor said there was no permanent damage and you would make a full recovery in a few weeks. He also gave me this topical cream called Arnica to treat the bruising. I heard this shit really works too."

"Well, give it here," I said with a slight chuckle. I couldn't laugh too hard or it would feel like a knife was poking me in the ribs.

"I got you. I put some on last night when we got here."

"How long did I stay at the doctor's?"

"For a few hours. He didn't feel you needed to stay overnight. I was glad I had chartered that plane because it was waiting for us and I didn't have to go through no bullshit. You were medicated up so you didn't know what the fuck was going on. This the first time you woke up since all this shit went down. I can finally relax a bit."

"Nico, I'll never forget what you've done for me."

"You better not. Now be still so I can put this cream on your face."

"Fine. I'll use the time to give you the play by play on how Maya's wicked ass orchestrated all this shit. Take your time with the cream 'cause this gon' take a minute."

As Nico began the process of nursing me back to health, I sat back to tell him the drama of how I went from LA to now saying "Hello, Brooklyn."

Maya
Prove You Wrong

"Cheers!" Devon and I said in unison as we clicked our champagne glasses in a hotel suite at the Peninsula Beverly Hills. When we left the burning house I knew I needed to shower and change clothes, and what better place to do so than a five star hotel, especially with my newfound riches. I hit the jackpot three times in one day.

"I can't believe I'm finally rid of Precious fuckin' Cummings. This has to be the best day of my life."

"Dang, ma, that chick really got under your skin. I ain't like her neither, but you hate her ass."

"*Hated*. She's past tense now. The bitch is dead, remember."

"I was there. I can't forget about her or Mike."

"Mike," I repeated out loud as if it was now hitting me that my brother was dead. He wasn't only dead but that I had killed him. "It's a shame what happened to Mike but he left me no choice."

"Right," Devon said, nodding his head and sipping on his champagne from the thousand-dollar bottle I purchased. "So what's next?"

"Next?" I asked, not knowing what next he meant.

"We got rid of Precious and Mike. Is the detective next? What are we doing?"

"We're not doing nothing. I don't think the detective will be a problem."

"Don't you think it will be best to get rid of all the loose ends?"

"Devon, let me do the thinking."

"I'm only considering your best interest. They will find the bodies in the house and eventually identify them as Mike and Precious. You know when that happens, Detective Moore will come sniffing around you."

"He can sniff all he wants, but making a case against me is something entirely different."

"It's on you, but hey, I'm more than willing to put the nail in his coffin."

"I'll keep that in mind," I said, standing up. "Enjoy the suite and I'll be in touch."

"Where are you going? You not staying to enjoy the suite with me?"

"Not tonight. I have to go."

"But I thought this was our celebratory evening together," Devon said, grabbing my wrist.

"And we did celebrate," I shot back, pulling my wrist from his grasp. "And now I'm leaving."

"That wasn't our agreement. You told me I would

be fully compensated for my services."

I reached in my purse and pulled out one of the thick roll of bills I had got from the briefcase. "This should be more than enough compensation," I said, tossing the cash in his lap.

Devon flipped his thumb through the hundred dollar bills. "Where did you get all this cash from? I'm sure you got some good pussy but not good enough for Supreme to hit you off with this kind of cash."

"Watch your mouth, Devon. And don't worry about where I got the cash, you've been compensated and that should be your only concern."

"The money is good, but I want a taste of that right there." Devon stuck out his thick pink tongue, pointing his finger towards my coochie. "I want what I was promised."

"So you rather get some pussy than all that cash?"

"Oh no, I'm keeping my money," he said, gripping the loot tightly. "But I'm getting both."

"You sound real confident in that."

"I am. We share a lot of secrets. I know you'll do the right thing. Come on, it won't be so bad. When I lay this pipe on you, trust you won't never want a piece of Supreme again."

"Is that right?"

"I promise you. Come over here and get a feel." Devon rubbed his hands over his crotch area as if I was going to come crawling over begging for the dick.

"I tell you what. Hold that thought. Supreme is expecting me and I don't want to raise any suspicions with all the shit that has gone down. But how about we meet back here tomorrow around the same time? You can show me what you holding down there." I walked right up on him and brushed my ass against him.

This fool had the audacity to grab my hand and press it against his dick. "Feel how hard you got my shit. You getting all this tomorrow night," Devon boasted.

I wanted to scream, "All what, you little dick nigga", but I needed him, so I kept my mouth shut. "That's right, baby, I can't wait. I'll see you tomorrow."

"Okay, and don't give Supreme none of my pussy until after I tap that ass. I want that shit nice and tight. Oh, and so you know, first thing tomorrow morning I'll be giving my boss a call to tell him I quit!" Devon hollered as I was walking out of the room. That comment stopped me dead in my tracks.

"Why in the hell are you quitting your job?"

"I'm tired of kissing that nigga's ass and talking all proper and shit around him like a corporate professional."

"Devon, you need your job."

"Not anymore. Shit, why I need to be on that nigga's payroll when I can be on yours?" he said, holding up the wad of cash I dropped in his hands. "Plus your benefits package is much better suited for my needs."

"That's a mistake," I warned.

"It's a mistake I'm willing to make."

"What are you going to tell Supreme?"

"The truth; that I got a better job offer and I'm moving on. I'm sure he won't have a problem replacing me. I mean he is Supreme."

"Have it your way."

"I plan to. We can work out my payroll schedule after I get done twisting your back out tomorrow."

All I did was smile at the dumb fuck before closing the door. If I had to stay in the room with Devon's nasty ass for one more minute, my head was going to explode. Getting thousands of dollars wasn't enough for the greedy fuck. He had to get between my legs too *and* quit his job. Now he looking at me to be his full source of income like I'm an ATM. It seemed that after I got rid of one problem there would always be another lurking around the corner, and the shit had me stressed.

When I got to my car I popped open the trunk and pulled out the briefcase. When I opened it up and saw the stacks of endless amounts of hundred dollar bills it was the only thing that brought me solace. "I'm a rich bitch!" I beamed.

I shut the briefcase back up and closed the trunk. And to think, if I hadn't been the curious chick I am, all that money would've burned up in flames with Mike and his beloved Precious. There were so many things I wanted to do with the money; for one, I wanted a fresh ride. I was tired of driving around in this same ol' Jaguar. I wanted some new hot shit. But before I went out splurging like a fool, I had to be extra careful. I didn't need anymore unnecessary heat.

After pulling up to the estate, I was disappointed because I didn't spot Supreme's car or his driver out front, and I was looking forward to seeing him. Ever since we had sex the other night, he was distant, as if he was purposely trying to avoid me. I knew it was out of guilt, but Supreme had to get over that shit.

The house was ghostly quiet and empty. When I turned on the lights the first thing that slapped me in the face was the life-size painted portrait of Precious and Supreme from their wedding day. It was as if Precious was haunting me in death. I wanted to take a knife and slash that shit in shreds. "I killed you! Would you die already and go away for good?" I screamed at the portrait as if Precious could hear me. As I was about to continue my hysterics I heard the door open. I quickly turned my head and saw Supreme coming in.

"Is everything alright? I heard yelling. Who were you screaming at?"

"That picture of Precious."

"Huh?" Supreme gave me a quizzical look like I was wilding out.

"I'm frustrated and hurt that Precious is gone. I want to yell at her, but since I can't I yelled at her picture. I know it sounds crazy, but all this anger has built up and I exploded. I feel betrayed that my best friend left and hasn't even reached out to me."

"I know what you mean," Supreme said, tossing his keys down on the table. "I can barely stand being in this house anymore. Everywhere I turn there is a reminder of her. So I know what you mean about exploding. Every second of each day I'm one second away from doing just that. I can't even stand being around people at this point."

"Is that why you've being avoiding me?" I asked, Supreme as he poured himself a drink.

"No, I've been avoiding you for a slew of other reasons."

"Like..."

"Like, I had no business having sex with you in the first place."

"Why?"

"Why? Do you really need to ask that question?"

"Because of Precious. At this point, what do we owe her? She left us both. How long are we supposed to mourn over her?"

"You mourn over people who are dead. My wife is very much alive which makes this shit that much more difficult to deal with."

"Do you want to deal with the fact that Precious left you, or do you want to hang on hoping she'll come back?"

"I don't know what the fuck I want." Supreme's face was riddled with emotions, from agitation, pain and confusion.

"You need to man up and figure it out."

"Excuse me?"

"You heard what the fuck I said. Your wife left you, accept it. You ain't the first man that had their wife leave them. Besides, you knew what type of woman Precious was before you married her."

"Now you saying I brought this bullshit on myself." Supreme stood up pounding on his chest.

"What I'm saying is there is truth to that adage, 'When you play with fire you might get burned'. Precious burned you, so get over it."

"Yo, fuck you, Maya!" I had Supreme raging and I was loving it.

"Fuck you too!" I said, pointing my finger in his face. I felt I needed to change up my approach and go hard core with Supreme. That sweet shit wasn't getting quick enough results with him.

"Get your fuckin' finger out my face."

"I'll do more than that. I'll get out your face for good. I don't need some confused nigga crying over a bitch that don't even want him and left for the next man. You can sit here and whine by yourself. Fuck you!" I stormed away and I felt Supreme grab my arm.

"Where the fuck you think you going?"

"Away from you and this dark cloud you got hanging over your head."

"No the fuck you ain't. You staying right here." Supreme clutched my face and stuck his tongue down my throat. He then lifted me up and sat me down on the white grand piano and ripped my panties off.

"You sure you want this pussy?" I murmured in his ear softly but clearly.

"You know I do," Supreme growled as he tore off my blouse and ravaged my neck. I smiled behind his back as he hands dug into my scalp, pulling on my hair. There was nothing more passionate than an angry fuck.

****

"Who the fuck is blowing my phone up?" I moaned, still half asleep. I put the pillow over my head hoping it would silence the noise but the ringing continued. "Supreme, turn my phone off, please." Within thirty seconds my cell was right back to the same shit and

I got no response from Supreme. I tossed the pillow off the bed and sat up looking around. Supreme was nowhere in sight and my phone was steady going off.

"I knew I shoulda left this shit downstairs last night," I said, getting out of bed to see who the stalker was on my line. "What the fuck is wrong with you?" I answered.

"What took you so long to answer the damn phone? You bet not be laid up with Supreme."

I took the phone away from my ear and stared at it, and then made sure the digits were correct across my screen before I responded. The nigga was still popping off at the mouth, and I walked over to the door to make sure Supreme wasn't lurking around anywhere. "Devon, why in the hell would you be blowing up my phone? You know Supreme could've easily looked at this shit and saw your number."

"Fuck that nigga! I don't work for him no more. Why would I care."

"You need to care. If he finds out we got dealings, our whole cover will be blown, you fuckin' idiot."

"Chill with the name calling. What time are you meeting me at the hotel?" Devon questioned, jumping to the next subject. "I already told my baby moms that I was working the all night shift and wouldn't be home, so we can spend the whole night together."

"Is that why you're blowing up my phone, not for no emergency shit but to see what time I'll be at the hotel?"

"Running up in some new, prime pussy is an emergency in my book. So what time should I be expecting you?"

"Listen Devon…"

"Un un, I don't want to hear none of that shit. Save the excuses. We have an understanding, one that I warned you not to back out of."

"Ain't nobody giving you excuses or backing out of shit."

"Then what were you about to say?"

"I was going to ask if you can get a room at another hotel."

"What's wrong with the place we have?"

"Supreme made a comment, and to be on the safe side, I think we should get a room somewhere else."

"What type of comment?"

"Devon, can you stop drilling me? Do you want to hook up tonight or not?"

"Of course. So what, I'll get the room and you'll reimburse me when I see you?"

"Yeah, I'll reimburse you." I couldn't believe this cheap motherfucker wanted some ass *and* wanted me to pay for him to get it.

"Cool. I'll call you later on with the hotel and room number."

"Can't wait." I shut my cell and tossed it on the bed. The thought of fuckin' that nigga had me ready to puke. How could I go from getting twisted out by super sexy Supreme to getting squashed by Devon?

"What has you in such deep thought?" Supreme asked, walking into the bedroom catching me off guard.

"Waking up seeing you were gone and wondering where you went."

"I got up early and went in my office to catch up

on some work."

"I thought maybe we were back to square one and you were avoiding me again."

"No, I understand your position on the situation. Precious left me, not the other way around. It's time for me to stop stressing over shit I have no control over."

"What does that mean for us?"

"I do have feelings for you, but I can't make you any promises."

"Can you at least promise to give us a chance?"

"A chance to what, be in a serious relationship?"

"What, is that so hard to imagine happening?"

"I don't want to take advantage of you, Maya. You're young and vulnerable. You went through all that bullshit with Clip, then you and Precious were close and I know her leaving has fucked you up, not to mention having someone like Mike for a brother. I don't want you to depend on me emotionally and I let you down too."

"I'm not worried about that."

"You should be. With Precious leaving, besides my love for Aaliyah, I don't think I have anything left to give."

"You say that now, but time heals all wounds. After Clip broke my heart I thought I was done with love until I fell for you, so it is possible."

"With youth brings optimism, but unlike you, I'm not a teenager anymore. It seems the more time passes the more enraged I become. You have too much ahead of you to become seriously wrapped up with me."

"Supreme, stop speaking for what I want and need. All I ask is that you give us a chance, nothing more nothing less. I'm not putting any guidelines or stipulations on our relationship. I just want to give us a try. Will you do that?"

"Yeah, we can do that."

"I'm going to make you so happy, you'll forget about all the pain in the past. I promise you," I said, wrapping my arms around Supreme's neck and embracing his lips with a wet kiss. Months ago I made up my mind that Supreme would be mine and there was no denying me. Only obstacle left was to take care of one last bump in the road, and its name was Devon.

****

After sealing the deal with Supreme I left out the house to get all the materials I needed for my evening with Devon. I spent all afternoon meticulously planning my shit out to go off without a hitch. As I was going over the operation in my head I heard my cell phone ringing. I eyed the caller ID and it was my nemesis.

"Hey, Devon, what's going on?"

"I was calling to give you the hotel information. I got us an official bungalow at The Beverly Hills Hotel."

"I bet that cost a pretty penny."

"Yeah, but since you footing the bill and money don't seem to be nothing but a thang to you, I went all out."

"How considerate, but I have to admit I'm getting very excited about being with you tonight."

'I bet. After you got a feel on how my dick hanging down there, you dying to throw that pussy on me. That shit better be tight too. You better not have given

Supreme none. I'll be able to tell if you did."

"I got you, baby. This will be one night you'll never forget."

"Cool. I'll see you soon."

I parked my car across the street, clutching my purse tightly as I sprinted towards the hotel. I spotted Devon's car in the parking lot and knew he was probably in the room rubbing his thumb-sized penis, imagining all the different positions he would fuck me in. When I knocked on the door Devon answered so quickly you would've thought he had been posted right beside the doorknob.

"What took you so long? I was about to start blowing up your cell."

"No need, I'm here now," I said, scooting past the wannabe cock blocker.

"What's all that you got in your hands?" Devon questioned at the Sephora bag I was carrying.

"Bath and body products. I wanted to spoil you with a hot bath, washing you from head to toe before we did the nasty."

"That sounds sexy."

"It is. I even have scented candles so you can be completely relaxed." I began taking out the candles and placing them on the table. "Did you order some champagne?" I asked not seeing any.

"It should be here any minute," Devon stated right as someone knocked at the door.

"You get the door, Devon, and I'll be in the bathroom setting up the candles." Devon didn't move and I wondered what he was waiting for. "What's the problem?"

"I need some money," he said, putting his hand out.

"Oh, stupid me. Here, this should cover it." I whipped out several hundred dollar bills and slapped them in his sweaty palms. While Devon was grinning, I hurried my ass in the bathroom not wanting to be seen by the waiter.

After I set up the candles I turned on the faucet in the Jacuzzi tub and poured in some L'Occitane foaming bath and oil. I heard the door shut and came out to the room and saw Devon holding two glasses.

"Here you go, baby. The waiter already poured it for us," Devon said, handing me my glass.

"Thank you, but go and check on the bath and make sure the water temperature is just right for you."

"Let me do that. Can't take any chances of that water burning my pretty skin," he said, rubbing his ashy arm. "Hold this for me." Devon handed me his glass.

"Of course. I'll be right here waiting for you." The second Devon was out of view, I opened my purse and poured the strong sedative in his glass of champagne. I added extra since Devon was a big motherfucker. I used my finger to stir it in quickly. "How's that bath coming?" I yelled, making sure Devon didn't pop out of the bathroom surprising me.

"I'm good. Come on in and bring the champagne." When I got in the bathroom, Devon had already stripped out of his clothes and squeezed his big ass in the Jacuzzi.

"You looking mighty comfortable," I commented in a flirty tone.

"I am. But, umm, I don't think there is enough room

for you to get in too."

"Don't worry, this is simply for your enjoyment. I'll get my pleasure by making you feel good."

"Maya, you my kind of woman. You pay for everything, wanna nigga to feel good, and you sexy as shit. I see our relationship lasting for a very long time."

"Me too. Now here, drink up." I handed Devon his glass. "But first a toast to the beginning of both of our futures."

"That's right." Devon gulped down his drink in one gulp. "Pour me some more, baby."

"Would love to, but before I do that, let me turn on some music."

"You making this real romantic."

"Oh fuck, I forgot the bottle in the bedroom. I'll be right back."

"Hurry up. I don't want your fine ass out of my sight."

I grabbed Devon's glass and happily refilled it and added some more of the sedative. I needed for him to be as relaxed as possible. Halfway asleep would be the easiest for me. "Here you go, baby. I hope I didn't keep you waiting too long."

"I'm good, but I want you to stand over there and strip for me. Grind to this music, get a nigga extra hard."

I damn sure didn't want Devon to have the pleasure of seeing me in the flesh, but I did need to stall so the sedatives could kick in. "You got it, you sexy black motherfucker." I stood a few feet from Devon and slowly began taking off one article of clothing at a time.

"Move them hips like Beyonce be doing when she grinding on stage," he directed, as if he was paying me Beyonce type money when this nigga wasn't kicking out loot for nada.

It had taken me over fifteen minutes to unbutton my silk blouse and the sedatives hadn't made a dent in Devon. I moved on to my crisp white pants, unzipping them just as slowly. Soon I found myself standing in my white lace bra and panties, slithering my body. Right when I was about to unclip my bra, I finally got some much needed indication that the shit was hitting home.

"What's wrong, Devon?" He was rubbing his eyes and bubbles were sliding down his face.

"I'm okay," he said, trying to shake off the drowsiness."

"Let me rub your shoulders, give you a little massage so you can feel real good."

"No need, I'm straight."

"Stop it. I want to make my man feel good." I went behind Devon and cemented my hands on his shoulders before he could protest any further. I felt his muscles getting weaker and his body wanting to collapse. "How does that feel?"

"That feels good," he mumbled, barely able to use his mouth to speak.

That's when I went in for the kill. I pulled out my syringe and filled it to the very top from the bottle of Potassium Chloride I had gotten earlier in the day. "Baby, it will all be over soon," I giggled as I plunged the needle in Devon's upper left shoulder. His body flinched but his muscles were too relaxed to react.

"What the fuck…" he stuttered.

I sat on the ledge of the Jacuzzi watching the anguish in Devon's eyes. "Devon, sweetie, you're having a heart attack. I know it's painful but soon you'll be in a more peaceful place. Better than that, after your dead and the coroner performs an autopsy they'll think your big ass died of natural causes."

Devon tried to lift up his arm and reach for my neck but it was a no go. He was entirely too weak at this point.

"Gotta go, and I won't be missing you or that little dick of yours." With the swiftness I gathered all my shit but made sure not to leave a clue that would lead to me.

"You brought this on yourself," I revealed, giving Devon a kiss goodbye on the forehead, leaving him for dead. "You thought this was your show to run. You left me no choice but to prove you wrong."

Precious
All Eyes On Me

"You're starting to look like your old self again," Nico said, standing in the doorway.

"Maybe on the outside but not on the inside." I stood in front of the mirror over the dresser able to truly see all my features and recognize my face for the first time in weeks. "Who knew that it took so long for bruises to heal after getting your ass beat?"

"But they're healed, that's the important thing. How is your rib?"

"Much better. Still some slight pain when I move, but at least I can walk without feeling as if I'm about to pass out. Thank you for nursing me back to health."

"Remember that, in case I ever need for you to do the same for me."

"Nico, I can promise you that if you ever need me, I'll be there no matter what."

"I believe you."

"It's the truth. I put that on everything."

"Precious, you don't have to convince me, I know your heart. Most people are fooled by that tough exterior but I know you."

"Then you also know I want to go home. I was too weak before but I need to be with my family."

"Are you sure you're ready?"

"Yes. I have to take care of a few things here, but after that I have to go straighten shit out with Supreme and see my daughter."

"Do you want to call him?"

"I thought about it so many times, but I have to handle this face to face. Then that letter Maya had me write…"

"What letter?"

"I was so busy telling you about the torture Maya put me through that I forgot to mention that bullshit letter the heifer had me pen."

"What did the letter say?"

"Basically she had me tell Supreme that I left him and I didn't want to be with him anymore."

"Word? I know he's fucked up behind that."

"Yeah, I'm sure Maya has taken full advantage, filling his head with all sorts of ridiculous shit."

"You mean shit about us?"

"Huh?"

"You don't have to 'huh' me, Precious. I know it was Supreme that put that hit out on me. You know, the one you came to New York to warn me about."

I let out a deep sigh and walked over to the bed to sit down. I was torn, but felt Nico deserved for me to be honest with him about a few things. "I guess I shouldn't ask how you found out."

"The same way I found Mike. I can find out pretty much anything if I ask the right questions to the right people."

"How long have you known?"

"It's been awhile now. When you gave me the warning, I put my sources on it and a few weeks later I got the info."

"You have to understand why I couldn't tell you who it was."

"He's your husband, I get that, which is the only reason I didn't try to retaliate against him. That, and I learned he pressed the pause button on the hit. But my question to you is, why did he want me killed?"

"Originally, I figured he harbored a lot of animosity for you trying to take my life which caused me to lose our baby. But I learned the real answer a few weeks ago."

"But you were on lock down a few weeks ago."

"Yeah, Maya was more than thrilled to inform me what Supreme had confided to her."

"Which was?"

"That he found out we had sex during the time I thought he was dead. I assumed it was our secret. Never did I think he would ever find out, but he did. That's what happens when the feds start recording your phone conversations."

"Leave it up to them motherfuckers to expose some

bullshit that has nothing to do with them. Now I see where the Maya thing fits in. You figure she's telling him you ran off with me."

"Exactly. And with me being MIA and our history, I can't blame him. I have to look him in his eyes so he knows I'm telling the truth. I also don't want him to give Maya any type of warning so she can plot and scheme her way out this bullshit she created."

"You think Supreme would get caught up in her lies?"

"One thing I've learned the hard way is to never underestimate that bitch."

"I feel you. So when are we breaking out?"

"We?"

"Yeah, we. I know you don't think I'm letting you go back to Cali by yourself."

"Nico, I can't bring you back to Cali with me. That would only further feed into the paranoia Supreme has about our relationship."

"Look, it ain't safe there for you. I ain't gonna let you walk into a danger zone by yourself."

"I won't be walking into a danger zone. Maya thinks I'm dead. She's probably dancing on top of a makeshift grave she created in my honor. When I make my presence known she will be caught totally off guard."

"Sorry, baby girl, I'm not willing to take that chance. Either we go together or you'll have to call Supreme and have him come meet you here. You need protection by someone you can trust, and that's me."

"I get it. But if you're going back to Cali with me, we have to do it my way."

"Don't we always have to do it your way?" Nico grinned.

"Whatever! But before we break out, I have to pay an old friend a visit, then we outta here."

"Who is that?"

"Nobody you know."

****

"Hi, welcome to Atomic Records. May I help you?" the middle aged, attractive receptionist asked.

"Yes, I'm here to see Jamal Crawford."

"Is he expecting you? Because he's in a meeting right now."

"No, he's not expecting me, but let him know that Precious Mills is here...*now!*" I gave the lady a half-ass smile and sat down on the typical black leather couch that all record companies seemed to have.

When I sat down, I noticed the receptionist staring at me but not picking up the phone. I was confused and annoyed by her hold up. "Excuse me, but is there a reason why you're not getting Jamal on the phone?"

"Well, Miss..."

"It's Mrs.," I interrupted.

"Mrs.," the lady sighed. "As I said, Mr. Crawford is in a meeting and I've been directed not to interrupt."

"I'm directing you to interrupt, and quite honestly it's not negotiable. Now call Jamal."

"I simply can't do that. I work for Atomic Records and Mr. Crawford. I have to follow his rules, not yours."

I chuckled out loud not in the mood to deal with

the bullshit. Although my face had pretty much healed and with makeup on you couldn't see a flaw, my mind, spirit and body were still fucked up. This chick sitting behind the desk was blocking on some 'this is my multi-million dollar company', when in all actuality she was just another employee. I had no time for this shit and was done playing with her.

"Listen," I began as I walked up on her. "This right here," I motioned my hands with the back and forth movement. "It's stopping right now. I don't have time to be playing paddy-cake with you. Get Jamal on the phone now, before I bust it over your head!"

The lady's mouth dropped, stunned by my threat, but I wasn't sure if she understood it was more than that. It was about to become her reality if she didn't speed up the tempo with her actions. I stood with my arms folded, staring the chick down, not flinching once. I counted to three in my head, and when she continued to act as if she was deaf, dumb and blind I bent over and seized her phone. "Now, are you going to call Jamal or are you going to be carried out this motherfucker in a stretcher?"

"I'm calling security right now!"

"You do that, but by the time they get here I would've busted your ass, spoke to Jamal and broke the fuck out. So like I said, what we doing?"

The lady picked up the phone slowly, and I wasn't sure what option she chose until she said, "Mr. Crawford, a Precious Mills is here to see you." She waited a few seconds and then hung up the phone. "Mr. Crawford said he would be right out."

"Now, was that so hard?" I grinned, flashing all thirty-two's.

I didn't even bother to sit back down. I began to walk back and forth waiting for Jamal, and by the time I got to my second turn back, Jamal had appeared. I instantly recognized the tall, reddish-skinned handsome man in the tailored coal gray suit. But no matter how distinguished Jamal grew up to be, in my mind he was still the bona fide hood genius from the projects I grew up in who popped my cherry.

"Precious, I'm surprised to see you," Jamal said, dryly. For some reason I was expecting a different greeting. There didn't have to be firecrackers and explosions, but at least a warm smile.

"Surprised or disappointed? I mean by the look on your face it definitely ain't happiness."

"Follow me. Let's go somewhere in private where we can talk."

I turned my head around and noticed the receptionist damn near falling out her chair trying to hear the words being exchanged between us. I rolled my eyes and picked up my pace so I could get down to it with Jamal. He led me to a conference room and we sat down across from each other at a table that could seat at least forty people.

"How have you been doing?" I asked, with a pleasant smile. I cared, but then I didn't care about the answer to that question. I had so much shit on my plate, but truth was I needed Jamal's help. And though I was itching to get right to it, I tried to play nice first.

"I doubt you care," he said, not trying to hide his true feelings. But this is how you play your game right?"

Okay, clearly Jamal was putting me on Front Street, airing my tactics out on the table. I was relieved, because again I was in no mood to dance around the topic. "You're right, Jamal, I don't care. From the looks of you, you're doing just fine. Maybe if my life wasn't so fucked up I would care, but that's not my circumstances."

"Yeah, last I heard you were missing. No one had spoken to you, not even your husband, Supreme."

"Jamal, I know who my husband is. You don't have to tell me his name," I said, becoming defensive. For the first time I looked down at Jamal's hand and saw that he was wearing a wedding ring. "Congratulations. I see you took the plunge."

He eyed down at the platinum band. "Yep, I'm a married man, and this time my fiancée didn't leave me at the altar, but then my first one technically didn't either. She was being murdered."

"Is that what the chip on your shoulder is about, Nina?"

"Of course! I know that you murdered her, Precious, and when the cops make their case, you're going to jail."

"Oh really? You're so sure about that?"

"Damn straight! I spoke to Detective Moore."

"Jamal, I'm not gonna even lie to you. I've done a lot of fucked up things in my life and I'm sure I'll do a lot more. But on everything I love, I didn't kill Nina. But let's be clear, she did deserve to die."

"Why should I believe you?"

"Because I know who did kill her. At the time, I thought she saved my life and I wanted to protect her. Now I know that she's just a manipulator."

"Kinda like yourself?"

"No...worse."

"When I came to your house that morning after learning Nina was dead, you looked me in my eyes and lied to me with a straight face. I believed you and you were lying to me."

"I told you I didn't kill Nina and that was the truth. I meant every word I said that morning. Nina was a loser. She didn't love you. What the fuck! You're married now. You're still hung up on that trick?"

"That's not the point. I trusted you as a friend and you deceived me."

"Oh please, Jamal, save the theatrics. We're talking about my life. You think I was willing to go to jail for a loser like Nina, who I didn't even have the pleasure of killing? Your so-called fiancée set me up. She wanted to kill *me*, and for what—so she could live out some fantasy, made up life with Nico. She was delusional and crazy. Those are two very dangerous components."

"How do you justify the way you live your life?"

"The same way you justify yours. Don't judge me, Jamal. That's not your right. You're a sinner just like me, and don't forget it."

The room went quiet, as if Jamal was soaking in all the words that we battled with. I knew I had blood on my hands, but I never killed anybody that I didn't feel deserved it. Was that my right to do? Well that was something I would have to settle with God.

"What do you need from me, Precious?" Jamal finally asked, breaking the silence. "I know you didn't come to see me because you missed me," he said sarcastically.

"You're right. I know it doesn't matter to you, but you are one of the very few people I respect, believe that." Jamal put his head down and didn't say a word. "Back to what I need from you: Have you ever been to an apartment that Nina had in Queens?"

"Queens? Nina didn't have an apartment in Queens."

"Yes, she did. Obviously you didn't know about it, like you didn't know about the apartment she kept on the West Side."

"You mean the one she kept your ex-fugitive boyfriend, Nico stashed in."

"Yeah, that one. Let's pause and backtrack for a moment because the petty hostility isn't giving me what I need."

"Why should I help you get what you need anyway?"

"Don't you want the person who is responsible for killing Nina to be brought to justice?"

"I find it hard to believe that you're doing all this to get justice for Nina, especially since you've made it very clear you're happy she's dead."

"You're right, it's not about Nina. Having her killer rot behind bars is an added bonus for you and the ultimate payback for me."

"I would like to see that happen, but again, I don't know about any apartment in Queens that Nina lived at. Did you run a search on her to check all previous addresses?"

"Yep, but no listings came up in Queens. Maybe the apartment wasn't actually in her name. I don't know, but I need that address," I said, tapping my fingernails on the mahogany conference table.

"Precious, where have you been? Are you back with Nico?"

"Where the hell did that come from?"

"Last I heard, Detective Moore said you were missing. You have a family, a daughter that was recently kidnapped, but instead of being in LA, you're here in New York searching for an address on Nina. Does this have something to do with Nico? I know you and him go way back. The two of you have some sort of twisted relationship that keeps you connected. I hope you're not throwing your life away to be with him."

"Are you done with the multiple questions, because Jamal, you don't have a clue to what you're talking about. Me coming here to see you and this search on Nina's address I'm doing, is all being done so I can be with my family again. Yeah, you right, Nico and I do share a deep connection. Some people may describe it as twisted, but it ain't nobody's fuckin' business. But best believe my family comes first."

"I think I might know."

"You don't know shit about me and Nico, Jamal."

"You're right, and I don't want to know. This is about Nina."

"Oh," I exhaled noisily, trying to calm down. "What do you know?"

"I have a box of Nina's belongings that I never got rid of." I gave Jamal a peculiar stare. "The same way I don't understand your love for Nico, you don't understand my love for Nina, and let's leave it at that," Jamal stated as if reading my mind, and I couldn't argue with what he said.

"I get it. Now continue."

"Nina had an address book that she would always keep with her. When she died, I went through it trying to find her relatives to let them know what had happened to her. She always told me she was estranged from her family, but of course I felt they needed to know that she had died."

"Did you get in contact with any of them?"

"No. There were a lot of names in there but none of them knew anything about Nina's family. A couple of people mentioned a person by the name of Terrell. They said it was her brother, who was dead. It was mind-boggling to me because Nina never even told me she had a brother who died. I apologize. I'm losing focus on the point I was trying to make."

"That's okay, take your time." It seemed like for the first time, at that moment I realized just how much pain Jamal was in over Nina's death and all the lies she told him. I never cared to understand or sympathize with his loss. Nina was less than zero in my eyes, but when I looked in Jamal's eyes, she was so much more.

"The point is, if I'm not mistaken I never threw that address book away. I believe it's in that box with some of her other belongings. It could be a stretch but maybe the Queens address is in there."

"Maybe so," I said, not wanting to get my hopes up too high. "I don't have any other options so it can't hurt."

"When I get off work, I'll go home and get the address book."

I leaned back in my chair and gave Jamal this look. It was this look I would get in my eyes ever since I was a little girl. It meant, *Don't fuck wit' me!*

"I know that look."

"I know you do. We did grow up together."

"How about I go get the address book now?"

"How about I think that's a plan?"

"I'm sure you do." Jamal smiled for the first time since I got here. "If you like you can come with me. Maybe meet me my wife."

"I'm sure she's lovely, but I'm not in the mood to pretend like I'm happy to meet someone. No offense."

"None taken. I hope you find everything you're looking for, Precious. It seems that in all the years that I've known you, I've never seen you happy."

"In my world, happy is a baby word, Jamal. All I want is for me and my family to stay alive. On that note, I need to go and so do you."

"Here, meet me at this address in an hour and I'll give you the book." Jamal jotted down the address on a piece of paper and handed it to me.

"Thanks again."

"Don't thank me yet. I don't even know if you're going to find what you're looking for."

"Even if the address isn't in there, thank you for

trying to help. You really didn't have to."

"Yes, I did. I want you to bring Nina's murderer down."

"You haven't even asked me who it is."

"I don't need for you to tell me. I have faith that you will handle it."

"I always knew you were a genius, baby. See you soon," I said, walking towards the door.

"Precious."

"Yeah?" I stopped and turned around before exiting.

"So you know, it does matter to me."

"I'm glad."

I left out of Atomic Records even more driven than when I went in. I wanted to find the apartment location in Nina's address book, but I wasn't going to give up even if I didn't. I needed my life back, the one that always seemed to be a few feet out of reach for me. I thought about what Jamal said, how he had never seen me happy. Long-term happiness did seem to elude me to the point I had accepted that it wasn't supposed to be a part of my life. I exploded into the world in the center of destruction, and I had been fighting for my rightful place ever since. Maybe the word 'happy' could find a place in *my* world. If I didn't feel I deserved it, my daughter damn sure did. And Maya or nobody else would deprive her of that. That meant I would have to do whatever needed to be done...even if all eyes are on me.

Maya
After All

"Supreme, I'm so happy Aaliyah is back home. This place wasn't the same without her," I said, bouncing her on my lap.

"I know, she lights up the whole house."

I watched as Supreme stared adoringly at his daughter. I knew he was thinking of Precious. He couldn't help it since it looked like Precious spit Aaliyah out. "Why don't the three of us go to the zoo today? It'll be fun." I didn't want to go to no damn zoo but I had to break up all that reminiscing Supreme was in the middle of.

"Sure, that would be fun. I know Aaliyah would love seeing all those animals."

"Great! I'll go get her dressed and we can get ready to go." I picked up Aaliyah and headed upstairs. When I reached the mid point I heard the doorbell ringing. "Supreme, are you going to get that?"

"Yeah, but I wonder who it could be and why the front gate security didn't let me know somebody was here," Supreme said, walking to the door.

I continued upstairs until the familiar voice made me stop and head back down.

"Detective Moore. I should've known it was you. You come to visit so often the security no longer feels the need to announce your presence."

"I'm flattered. Can I..."

"Of course, come in."

"Thank you." I heard Supreme close the door as I reached the bottom step. "Well look it here, it's Maya Owens. I see you're stepping into that mother role with ease. That baby gets cuter every time I see her."

"Hello, Detective Moore. As always, it's a pleasure to see you," I mocked.

"Same here."

"Detective, we were on our way out, so what brings you here today?" Supreme asked.

"I have some news that I wanted to share with both of you."

"Did you find out where Precious is?" Supreme couldn't even control himself from wanting to know the whereabouts of his beloved Precious. Even with the bitch dead, she was still living in our house.

"No, but I know one place she is not."

"Where?" I wanted to stay out of the conversation but my anxiousness got the best of me.

"With your brother, Mike Owens," Detective Moore turned to me and said.

Supreme grabbed his arm and turned him back around. "What makes you so sure?"

"Because Mr. Owens perished in a fire a few weeks ago."

"What? What happened?" Supreme questioned, becoming animated.

"It seems he had been staying at a house in Calabasas and a horrific fire started, and not by accident," he added, cutting his eyes in my direction. I kept swinging Aaliyah on my hip as I didn't peep his shade.

"It was arson?"

"Yes, it was. The whole house was pretty much destroyed."

"Then how are you sure it was Mike that died in the fire?"

"It took a long time, but the medical examiner was able to get a partial fingerprint, and of course they ran it threw the system. With Mike having a criminal record his name came up. His body was found in the basement. Whoever set the fire shot him first."

"That motherfucker finally got his!" Supreme said, slapping his hands together.

"Maya, you don't seem surprised by what happened to your brother."

"Should I be? I'm sure with the life he lived he made a lot of enemies."

"I can't believe that motherfucker was living right here in California. What the fuck was he sticking around for?"

"Mr. Mills, that's interesting because I was trying to figure out the same thing. I was hoping Maya here could help me."

"How can I help? Like I told you, I haven't had any contact with my brother."

"You did tell me that. Mr. Mills, you can rest a bit easier knowing that the man who brought so much tragedy to your family is now dead."

"Damn, straight! But there goes another dead lead when it comes to finding Precious. I'm glad he doesn't have her, but I do want to know where she is."

"Was Mike staying in the house by himself?" I asked.

"I'm sorry, Maya, what did you say?" Detective Moore put his finger behind his ear and leaned forward.

"I said, was anybody else in the house with Mike?"

"Not that we know of. Again, the house was burned pretty bad, but they didn't find any other bodies."

That can't be! Precious died in that fire too! Maybe her body was burned so bad that there wasn't any sort of trace. But there would have to be something left. Or maybe Detective Moore is playing games with me trying to get me to tell on myself. Only the person who set the fire would know that another body shoulda been found. Yeah, Detective Moore is definitely trying to set me up. He's been suspicious of me from day one but can't get anything to stick. He is counting on me to slip up and put the nail in my own coffin. Nah, you gon' have to come better than that. If you sticking to the story that only Mike died in the fire, than so am I.

"Detective, I appreciate you coming over here and informing us about Mike."

"Of course. I'm sorry we haven't been able to find any leads on your wife. I hope you haven't given up finding her."

"Of course not, but I also can't stop living my life. It seems that there hasn't been any foul play and her life isn't in jeopardy, so I have to assume she left on her own free will."

"It would seem that way, but again, I'll keep my eyes open. With the way the pieces to this puzzle are coming together, anything is possible."

"Maya... Maya..."

"Huh?" I finally answered Detective Moore, snapping out of my deep thoughts.

"I guess you got something heavy on your mind," the detective pried on the sly. "Are you going to be okay?"

"I appreciate your concern, but I'll be fine."

"Good, I'm sure you will. What I wanted to tell you was that we tried to get in contact with your mother so she could claim your brother's remains, but we haven't had any luck."

"I'll take care of it."

"Here's my card, if your mother has any questions."

"Thanks," I said, snatching it out his hand.

"I'll be going now. I don't want to overstay my welcome but I'm sure I'll be back. Like you said, Mr. Mills, I'm a frequent visitor."

I stood on the side watching Supreme escort Detective Moore to the front door. That man truly made my skin crawl and I regretted not letting Devon kill him before I took him out. Now with Devon dead I had nobody to finish off the job. But as long as I played it cool I was untouchable. I had gotten rid of all the loose ends. Everybody who had any dirt on me was dead. I had to remain focused and calm. I was this close to having everything I wanted. Supreme was still in love with Precious, but slowly he was accepting the fact that she left him and their baby. As much as he loved her, Supreme would never be able to forgive such betrayal. And now with Precious dead, he would go to his grave never knowing otherwise.

****

I strolled down Rodeo Drive on a beautiful afternoon, ready to shop away all the memories of yesterday's visit from Detective Moore. Before I got started, I decided to make a pit stop at the Peninsula Spa. I needed a top-of-the-line manicure so my hands would be stunning as I handed over Supreme's credit card to the cashier. Then my pedicure had to be flawless so when I tried on pricey stilettos my feet would be the perfect decoration.

When I arrived at the spa, it was completely quiet. Since it was a one-person nail salon it cut out any hoopla. I sat down to get my Pacific Coast Manicure and watched the standard California bleach blond with over enhanced silicon tits sip champagne while getting a signature pedicure. It was a Reflexology, an herbal foot bath, and jasmine oil massage. It was a cool $155, but it was worth it for seventy-five minutes of foot heaven.

"I love your purse," the bleached blonde babbled between sips of her bubbly. The Chanel, metallic calfskin bowling bag I was carrying was official. I couldn't even front on that.

"Thank you. It was a gift from my boyfriend."

"Your boyfriend has great taste. He seems like a keeper."   "I would have to agree, on both."

"Well you better hurry up and try to marry him while you can. We're in Beverly Hills, young lady. These women are treacherous. I'm in real estate, and although business is booming for me, with this economy being such a mess some of my competitors are willing to do anything, and I mean, *anything!*" she stressed, "To close the deal, if you know what I mean," she said, and winked her eye.

"I know what you mean. It's pretty competitive in my business too. Women are willing to kill to get what they want," I laughed as if joking, and the lady laughed back, having no idea how serious I was.

"Well, if you ever do get that man down the aisle, and when you're ready to start a family, call me. I sell the most luxurious homes money can buy. Whatever the request, I guarantee I can fulfill it." She reached in her purse and pulled out one of her business cards.

"No, thanks. I appreciate the offer, but we already live in a beautiful gated estate in Beverly Hills."

"Work it out! Kudos to you for learning at a young age to use what the good Lord above gave you to get what you want."

"I'm trying."

"With the bag you're carrying and an estate in Beverly Hills, darling, you're more than trying, you've seemed to have figured it all out."

I was really enjoying the fake white girl bullshit with this lady and chuckled, then found myself imitating her phony hand gestures and the whole nine. I could see how chicks like Lil' Kim and them ended up 100% plastic after getting caught up in the allure of Holly*weird*.

"Hold on a moment, I have a call," I said, sounding all extra valley girl like the realtor did. "Hello," I said, speaking into my Blue Tooth."

"Bitch, you shoulda stayed in that hotel room until you knew my black ass was dead!" I thought my heart had jumped out my chest when I heard Devon's voice on the other end of the phone.

"Devon, is that you? You fell asleep the last time I saw you and I haven't been able to get in touch with you. I was worried," I said, trying my best to play this shit off with him.

"Is that him on the phone?" I caught the realtor chick mouthing as I turned my head in her direction. She was cheesing from ear-to-ear while pointing her finger at my Blue Tooth. I smiled back and nodded my head 'yes', wanting to quickly shut her down. My five minutes of pretending to be a Hollywood socialite were over. This phone call kicked me back into hood life reality quickly.

"Shut the fuck up with that lying, Maya! You know fuckin' well I wasn't sleep. You drugged me and then tried to poison me, you triflin' bitch! Luckily, I'ma big nigga, and I had the strength before that shit kicked all the way in to pick up the phone and get some help."

"Devon, I don't know what you're talking about,

but I'm glad you're okay."

"No you're not. You wanted me dead, just like your brother and Precious. I can't wait to tell Supreme how you murdered his wife."

"Devon, calm down. There is no need for threats." The palms of my hands were sweaty and my fingers were shaking. The lady gently pressed down on them to stop it, but it wasn't helping.

"Ho, this ain't no threat. I'ma fuck your schemin' ass up!"

"Wait, I can get access to a lot of money—it's yours." The phone went silent and I knew Devon's greedy ass was considering what I had said. "I'll give you a million dollars," I added, although there was much more in the suitcase I took from Mike, but he didn't need to know that."

"How do I know you ain't playing games, Maya?"

"Because you're holding all the cards," I spoke softly, not wanting anybody to hear what I was saying. "All I ask is you give me a week to get the money."

"Fuck that! You got three days or I'm going to Supreme."

"Devon, a million dollars is a lot of money. I need some more time. I'm good for it. If you blow up my spot with Supreme then you'll have nothing. We will both end up in jail and you'll be broke," I whispered.

"Five days. That's all your evil ass gets. I swear if you don't have my million dollars by then, I guess we'll both be serving life sentences." Then the phone went dead.

"Is everything okay?" the realtor asked a few minutes after she noticed my mouth was no longer yapping.

"I'm fine. I just got some unexpected news."

"Good, I hope."

"What's your name again?"

"It's Kitty."

"Kitty, let me get your card. I think I will need your services after all."

Precious
Last Bitch Standing

From the moment Jamal placed Nina's address book in my hands I had been consumed with it for the last four days. She had so many names and numbers you would've thought it was the yellow pages. There were several addresses in Queens listed, and I had spent two days visiting those places and none of them were the spot. I got tired of knocking on doors and coming up with bullshit excuses as to why I was at their front entry. Based on the description Mike had given me, I knew most of the spots I rolled up on couldn't have been the correct place, but I was so desperate I would try regardless. Mike said the place was in a low-key neighborhood, but I would pull up on a block with a gang of dealers kicking it on every corner rolling dice knowing, shit wasn't going to be in my favor.

Besides the address book, Jamal also gave me a pair of keys he found inside a jewelry box Nina had. Again, he wasn't sure but he thought that maybe they were the keys to the apartment I was looking for. When I would go to certain spots that seemed to fit the bill and I knocked on the door and no one would answer, I would try the keys but zilch was opening up so far.

After staying up day and night, I was finally down to the last five pages of the book. There were four addresses listed for Queens. If none of these worked, then I would have to come up with another plan because nothing was going to stop me from bringing Maya all the way down.

Knock! Knock! Knock!

"Come in, Nico."

"Have you found what you're looking for yet? I'm getting concerned."

"So am I. I only have four addresses to go. If this don't work, I don't know what I'm going to do."

"We'll stick to the plan, go to LA and tell Supreme what the hell that crazy ass Maya did to you."

"Of course I'm going to do that, but I want Maya in jail forever. I really want her dead, but I'm a mother and Aaliyah needs me in her life not locked up behind bars."

"That's smart thinking, Precious."

"Yeah, but I have to get the evidence I need to seal her fate."

"But you can tell the police she was the mastermind behind all that bullshit and that she kidnapped you."

"True, but you know she's going to place all the blame on Mike, and with him dead, it's a gamble and she might get off. I'm sure she'll get some slimy attorney who will insinuate that I'm making the whole story up out of jealousy because of her relationship with Supreme. Trust me, with this shit being more bizarre than a daytime soap opera, combined with my shady past, I need the smoking gun to make sure Maya is officially done, case fuckin' closed."

"I understand all that and you know I love having you around. But you need to get home to your daughter and your husband. The longer you have Maya around your family, the worse it's going to be."

"True. Well then, we need to check out these last four addresses, and even if we come up short, tomorrow I'll be going home."

"Now you're talking, so let's go."

****

It felt as if Nico and I had been driving around in circles all day, or better yet, at a standstill in afternoon traffic, and it had all been in vain. We had three strikes in a row, and I was drained but undeterred. I wasn't expecting to hit gold in my search, but I did want to be able to say that I tried every option given to me. I laid my head back on the reclined seat gazing out the window, finding one positive thing in this entire situation. This time tomorrow, I would be holding my baby girl. Knowing that put a smile on my face.

As Nico turned the corner onto the block of a quaint street in the Astoria, Queens neighborhood, the longing feeling of holding my child again was put on pause. "This is it," I said, as a calmness came over me.

"Huh?" Nico turned to me like he didn't understand

or hear what I said.

"This is it. This is where the apartment is." I sat straight up in the seat looking for the address that was written on the second to last page in the book. It simply had 'Mildred' as the name with the address underneath, but I knew this was the spot. No matter how hard I had tried to make myself get that feeling of hope when I had pulled up to a minimum of twenty-five apartments in the last few days, none of them gave me that, until now.

"What makes you sure?"

"I'll put it like this: Remember when we were together and my gut told me you were fuckin' around on me? My gut instinct is doing the same shit right now about this apartment."

"I can't knock that shit."

"No you can't, now pull over. There's the building," I said, pointing straight ahead."

When we got out of the car I practically ran to the entrance of the brownstone building. The door was locked and I reached in the back pocket of my jeans and pulled out the set of keys. I knew this was do or die time. I put the first key in the lock but it wouldn't open the door. I could hear Nico letting out a disappointing sigh. He knew how desperately I wanted this shit to work out in my favor and he didn't want me to hit another dead end—and he wouldn't have to. When I put the second key in, that shit turned and the lock popped as if I had been opening this very same door all my life.

"Motherfuckin' right!" Nico pumped his fist in the air

sharing in my enthusiasm.

"It's apartment Number 2. There seems to be one apartment on each floor so it must be one flight up." We skipped up the stairs, and when I got to the apartment that had #2. I put my ear to the door to make sure no one was there. Nico did the same thing and neither of us heard anything suspicious. I put the first key in, and again that shit opened right the fuck up.

Surprisingly, the joint was in great condition. It was apparent that whoever Mike had checking up on the spot was on top of their job. The two bedroom apartment was sparsely furnished but very clean. The place wasn't huge but it was spacious enough that the gun could've been stashed in numerous places.

"Where do you want to start?" Nico asked, reading my thoughts.

"I'll take the first bedroom, you take the one in the back and we'll work our way out front."

"Sounds like a plan. Let's get to it."

When I went into the bedroom, the first thing that caught my eye was a picture on the nightstand. It was Nina standing next to a young man that I assumed was her brother, Terrell. The resemblance was undeniable—the thick black eyebrows, rich brown complexion, full lips and high cheekbones, gave both model-type features. Now I understood what Mike meant about all the women this cute, young nigga had. Maya didn't stand a chance. He had 'heartbreaker' stamped on his forehead.

I put the photo down and got down to business. I looked under the bed, mattress, drawers, closets, behind the television, anyplace that could remotely conceal a gun. I thought finding the correct apartment would be the hardest part, but finding the gun was already proving to be an exhausting chore.

"Any luck?" I heard Nico ask after I had been up down, and around, back on my hands and knees for over an hour, not missing a crack.

"No, you neither."

"I searched the bedroom and the bathroom, now I'ma search the living room and kitchen."

"I'll help because it's definitely not in here."

Nico started in on a hardwood floor check, making sure there weren't any secret compartments underneath us. I began with the couches, and again coming up empty. After what seemed like an eternity we took it to the kitchen with no such luck. After over three hours of nothing, I was running on empty.

"Maybe Mike was lying and he didn't hide the gun here."

"I didn't get that vibe from him, plus I can feel that gun. It's here, I'm telling you. It's crazy, but I think after you have kids, if you listen carefully, your female intuition triples."

"I'm really scared of you now. Women don't need no more extra power over us."

"Nico, I'm being serious."

"Shit, me too."

We both fell back on the couch, tired as hell. "Never did I expect this to turn into a real life treasure hunt game. I figured it wouldn't take us no more than fifteen minutes to find this damn gun—thirty at the most. The way it's looking it's turning to an all day and night affair," I said, looking at the bookshelf against the wall.

"You got that shit right. Baby girl, you know I would stay and search this place for as long as you like, but I'm becoming skeptical about the information Mike gave you."

I got up while Nico was talking, halfway listening and halfway remembering things Mike had said to me: *"...It's proper resting place...My gift to Nina...Me stashing it at the spot Terrell would hold down for her was like me putting the shit to rest..."*

I looked intently at the cream-colored photo album with the gold script words engraved on the front that read "Nina and Terrell Douglas". I smiled and picked it up. It was so heavy I almost dropped it.

"Precious, what are you doing? We don't have time for you to be looking at some photos, we have to find the gun, and looking at that clock on the wall, we're running out of time."

"Our work here is done. We can go now."

"You're giving up? We haven't found the gun, unless you believe I'm right and Mike didn't stash it here."

"It's here. Look inside," I said, opening the bootleg photo album. The first two pages had photos, then the third page was blank, and when you turned it, there was a deep opening, and sitting pretty was that smoking gun.

"How did you know? I would've turned everything in this place upside down and still not touched that fuckin' album."

"One, getting into Mike's twisted mind, and two, that female intuition I keep stressing."

"Your odds are on point. Now let's break the fuck outta here. We have a flight to catch in the morning."

****

When our flight landed at LAX on Saturday afternoon, I was thrilled to be coming home. I replayed the million questions Supreme would have for me when I walked through the door and what my response would be. Then I wondered if Maya would be there and visualized the stunned look on her face when she saw the person she left for dead was not only alive, but had the weapon that would send her away doing football numbers. Then, most importantly, my baby.

"How are you feeling?" Nico asked, squeezing my hand as we sat in the back seat of the chauffeur driven car.

"I'm fine."

"No you're not. There's nothing wrong with being nervous, Precious."

"I didn't say there was."

"You didn't have to."

"You know me too well, Nico."

"You're right, I do. I want you to know that being with you these last few weeks have been wonderful. It was like old times you know, besides the fact we weren't sharing a bed," he joked.

"Yeah, that does a make a difference. But seriously, I enjoyed spending time with you too. I'll never forget that not only did you save my life, but you nursed me back to health. Our bond is thick, baby."

"It is and it always will be. But I have to let go. You don't belong to me anymore. You're another man's wife and you have to go home and claim your family.

"The way you know me so well, I know you too.

This is difficult for you but you're being such a man about it, and it makes me love you that much more."

Nico lifted my chin and placed the most endearing kiss on my lips. "My beautiful, Precious. No longer are you just radiant on the outside, but you're finally just as radiant on the inside. I always knew you had it in you."

I kept my composure refusing to shed a tear. This was no time to soften up and be weak. I was about to enter a territorial war zone with Maya and my shit had to be solid as steel. There would be time for me to rejoice in my newfound inner peace after I brought Maya the fuck down. When the car started driving up to the estate, I couldn't wait.

"I wonder why the gates are open and there is no security out front. That's strange," I commented.

"It could be the middle of a shift change or something like that."

"True." When we drove up to the driveway the only car I noticed was a silver big body Benz parked in front. "I wonder whose car that is."

"You'll find out shortly."

"Are you sure you don't mind waiting in the car? I feel bad."

"Don't. You didn't want me coming at all."

"It's not that, it's Supreme's paranoia about us."

"Precious, you don't have to explain. We've been through this. All I want to do is make sure that you get home safely to your family. I'll wait here for a little while until I know you have things under control. Then I'll leave."

"Thank you, Nico."

"Stop with all that. Make me proud. Go in that house and let everybody know the queen is back!"

I got to the entrance and rang the doorbell. I could hear heels clicking on the marble floors and my heart was racing. This was my moment and I planned on embracing every second of it.

"Hello there, you must be my three o'clock appointment." The extra bubbly blonde greeted me after opening the door. "Are you alone, or is your husband coming in?" she said, looking over my shoulders at the car Nico was in the backseat of.

"Who are you and what appointment are you talking about?"

"I'm Kitty, the realtor. It's a pleasure to meet you," she said, extending her hand. I brushed her hand away because I was afraid I would break each bony finger if I got a hold of them.

"Well what do we have here? Is there a problem, Mrs. Hughs?"

"My name ain't Mrs. Hughs. It's Precious Mills and I own this house with my husband, so get the fuck out!"

"There is no need to take that tone with me. I was hired by Mr. Mills' attorney to sell this house. This is its first day on the market..."

"And its last," I cut in.

"I don't even know you. The only woman I know Mr. Mills to be involved with is his girlfriend, Maya

Owens. She was the sweet young lady that introduced me to Mr. Mills."

"And where might they be? Are they inside right now?" I asked, mowing my way past the silly broad.

"Excuse you!" she snarled, patting her tweed suit.

"Where is Supreme?"

"Who?" she asked, revealing a heavy southern accent that she had been covering up thus far.

"Mr. Mills, where is he?"

"I have no idea. All I know is that they wanted to start fresh in a new place and moved."

"Where, to a new house in Beverly Hills?"

"No, out of state."

"Out of state? Are you sure?"

"Yeeeessss," she said, singing the word. "I'm very sure."

"But you don't know which state?"

"No I don't, because the only place I sell houses is here in Beverly Hills. I have no idea where they went, but I'm sure they're going to be just fine."

"Lady, get the fuck out my house!"

"This isn't your house."

"Take a good long look at that portrait on the wall right there," I pointed my finger firmly in case the dizzy chick had vision problems.

"Well, I'll be damned! That is you! What a beautiful picture. Are you some sort of model?"

"Listen, I'm in a very bad mood right now. So get your skinny, plastic ass out of my face before I break it."

"Precious, what's going on?"

"Are you Mr. Hughes? I think you need to calm

your wife down."

"Did you just not see the picture on the wall? I'm not Mrs. Hughes. My name is Precious Mills and my husband is Supreme AKA Xavier Mills. Now remember that as you're walking out the door and don't ever come back!"

"But I have a three o'clock appointment. My clients are my first priority."

"Even before saving your own life?" I balled up my fists so she completely comprehended my question.

"I'll be going now. But I will be calling Mr. Mills' attorney and informing him of what took place today."

"Do that...after you get the fuck out."

"Goodbye. Oh, and here is my card in case you change your mind," she said, handing it to Nico. "Again, my name is Kitty and I sell the most luxurious houses in Beverly Hills," were her parting words as she closed the door.

"What the hell was that about?"

"Supreme has vanished with my daughter and Maya is with them."

"What?"

"Yes. That was some realtor that Maya introduced Supreme to, and he hired her to sell our house before they left town, to start fresh, as Kitty put it. But that's cool. I will turn this motherfucker upside down and find my husband and child. Maya can play if she wants to, but I will be the last bitch standing!

P.O. Box 912
Collierville, TN 38027

A KING PRODUCTION

www.joydejaking.com
www.twitter.com/joydejaking

ORDER FORM

Name:

Address:

City/State:

Zip:

QUANTITY	TITLES	PRICE	TOTAL
	Bitch	$15.00	
	Bitch Reloaded	$15.00	
	The Bitch Is Back	$15.00	
	Queen Bitch	$15.00	
	Last Bitch Standing	$15.00	
	Superstar	$15.00	
	Ride Wit' Me	$12.00	
	Ride Wit' Me Part 2	$15.00	
	Stackin' Paper	$15.00	
	Trife Life To Lavish	$15.00	
	Trife Life To Lavish II	$15.00	
	Stackin' Paper II	$15.00	
	Rich or Famous	$15.00	
	Rich or Famous Part 2	$15.00	
	Rich or Famous Part 3	$15.00	
	Bitch A New Beginning	$15.00	
	Mafia Princess Part 1	$15.00	
	Mafia Princess Part 2	$15.00	
	Mafia Princess Part 3	$15.00	
	Mafia Princess Part 4	$15.00	
	Mafia Princess Part 5	$15.00	
	Boss Bitch	$15.00	
	Baller Bitches Vol. 1	$15.00	
	Baller Bitches Vol. 2	$15.00	
	Baller Bitches Vol. 3	$15.00	
	Bad Bitch	$15.00	
	Still The Baddest Bitch	$15.00	
	Power	$15.00	
	Power Part 2	$15.00	
	Drake	$15.00	
	Drake Part 2	$15.00	
	Female Hustler	$15.00	
	Female Hustler Part 2	$15.00	
	Female Hustler Part 3	$15.00	
	Female Hustler Part 4	$15.00	
	Female Hustler Part 5	$15.00	
	Female Hustler Part 6	$15.00	
	Princess Fever "Birthday Bash"	$6.00	
	Nico Carter The Men Of The Bitch Series	$15.00	
	Bitch The Beginning Of The End	$15.00	
	Supreme...Men Of The Bitch Series	$15.00	
	Bitch The Final Chapter	$15.00	
	Stackin' Paper III	$15.00	
	Men Of The Bitch Series And The Women Who Love Them	$15.00	
	Coke Like The 80s	$15.00	
	Baller Bitches The Reunion Vol. 4	$15.00	
	Stackin' Paper IV	$15.00	
	The Legacy	$15.00	
	Lovin' Thy Enemy	$15.00	
	Stackin' Paper V	$15.00	
	The Legacy Part 2	$15.00	
	Assassins	$11.00	

Shipping/Handling (Via Priority Mail) $7.50 1-2 Books, $15.00 3-4 Books add $1.95 for ea. Additional book.
Total: $_____FORMS OF ACCEPTED PAYMENTS: Certified or government issued checks and money Orders, all mail in orders take 5-7 Business days to be delivered

Made in the USA
Las Vegas, NV
28 February 2021

18737702R10132